Lady Rample Spies a Clue

Lady Rample Mysteries:
Book Two

Shéa MacLeod

Lady Rample Spies a Clue
Lady Rample Mysteries: Book Two

Printed in the United States of America.

Cover Art by Amanda Kelsey of Razzle Dazzle Designs
Editing by Alin Silverwood
Formatting by PyperPress

This one's for Julie M.
Because she loves Devon as much as I do.

Chapter 1

"You're going to kill us all!"

"Don't be dramatic." I gave Aunt Butty the side-eye as she clutched her hat firmly to her head. Today's monstrosity was ivory felt covered in so many pearls it was a wonder she could hold her head upright. An enormous, white ostrich feather poked wildly from the back. I hadn't the heart to tell her the tip had been crushed against the roof of my beloved motorcar.

"Eyes on the road!" she shrieked, bosom heaving.

I did so in time to discover a hedgerow looming rather closer than I was comfortable with. Yanking the wheel hard to the right, I managed to avoid scraping the paint of the cobalt blue Mercedes Roadster—a gift from my late husband, Lord Rample. Unfortunately, I nearly took out a lorry coming the other direction. The driver blared his horn and shook a fist as he rumbled past.

"We're fine, Aunt." If my heart had lodged itself somewhere in my throat, I'd never admit it. Instead I gave her a bright smile and forced myself to relax my grip on the steering wheel. "Not much further now. I can see the church spire in the distance." Our destination, the village of Stickleberry in Devon, was practically just around the corner. In fact, I could already smell the fresh sea air.

"Too far for my taste," Aunt Butty muttered. I noticed she hadn't let go of the door handle or her hat. "And you don't fool me one bit, Ophelia."

I'd no doubt of that. Aunt Butty knew me far too well. She was my favorite—if only—aunt, after all, and—when I was sixteen—had saved me from a dastardly dull life and ushered me into the realm of the glitterati. If anyone in this world knew me, it was her.

Two ornate wrought iron gates appeared just ahead. They were firmly placed in an ancient stone wall swathed in ivy. Next to the gates, a neatly carved stone newly imbedded in the wall declared this to be Wit's End.

"There, you see. As I said." I tooted the horn as we approached, and the gates swung open almost as if by magic. That is, if magic were powered by a uniformed gateman with an impossibly enormous handlebar moustache and eyebrows that could have had their own post code.

He waved us through with a flourish, and I zipped up the drive, winding beneath the spread of oak trees. It was as if we were passing through a long, green tunnel. Green-tinted dappled light filtered through the leaves, creating a dream-like world that beckoned us onward. The cool, shaded air was a welcome relief to the stifling summer heat. It was unseasonably warm even for July.

We burst out of the tunnel and into full daylight once again.

"Good gracious, it's magnificent, isn't it?" Aunt Butty stopped clutching at her hat to eyeball the edifice looming above us.

The manor was Georgian, whitewashed, and gleaming. A small portico supported by simple, elegant pillars stood guard over the front steps. Small, square windows glinted like jewels in the sun. We swept up the drive, around a large fountain containing a fat, naked cherub spewing a stream of water from his nether regions and came to a stop by the front door in a spray of gravel.

Aunt Butty let out a sigh of relief and leaned back weakly against the seat. I managed to hold back a snort at her theatrics.

The manor door itself was the same white as the stone walls, as if it could blend into the facade. Wisteria—only a few of the lush, purple blooms left this late in the season—trailed up and over the portico before spilling down in an elegant swath. The door swung open and a black-garbed butler stepped out and strode across the drive, his pace even, unhurried. As if there were all the time in the world. He swung open the passenger door for my aunt even as my own opened and a liveried chauffeur grinned down at me.

"My lady. May I assist you?" He had a marked accent, vaguely European, and a dimple in his cheek. I imagine he had half the ladies of Stickleberry swoony, despite the distrust of country fold for anything foreign.

He helped me from the car with all the deference due my station and then some. Before I knew it, I found myself standing in front of the stiff, unapproving butler. His collar was so starched, it was a wonder he didn't put his own eye out.

"Welcome to Wit's End." He said it with an absolutely straight face and with as much flourish as one might announce Buckingham Palace or Balmoral.

"What a dashed odd name for a manor house," Aunt Butty muttered. "Harry must have been feeling a bit cheeky. I approve."

"Ophelia, Lady Rample. And this is my aunt, Lady Lucas." Technically speaking, Aunt Butty was a mere Mrs. Trent. It was the second of her three husbands who'd been Lord Lucas, but my aunt much preferred the title—not to mention the second husband—and used it when she could, whether it was hers or not. After all, as she put it, Lord Lucas was dead as a doornail and without heirs, so who was to complain?

The butler bowed deeply. "I am Jarvis."

"Of course, you are," my aunt muttered. I nudged her with my elbow, and she shot me an aggrieved look.

There was more bowing and scraping nonsense before we were ushered inside while the chauffeur drove away with my car. I did hope he treated her right. She was a thing of beauty. A single scratch and I would have his head, dimple or no dimple.

The front door led directly into a large foyer with a smooth floor of white marble shot through with gray. Directly in front of us was a wide, sweeping staircase leading upward, the polished wooden treads covered in a red and gold carpet runner that looked practically new. To the right was an ornately carved mahogany hall tree complete with bench and cloudy antique mirror. To the left was a tall pillar in the same marble as the floor with a white bust of some famous person or other perched on top. It looked like possibly Mozart, but it could have been any number of big-wigged historical gentlemen. In any case, the bust was currently graced by a tri-horn hat tipped cockily over one eye.

We were turned over to the housekeeper who ushered us upstairs in a jangle of keys and swish of crinolines. Really, who wore crinoline these days? It was 1932, for mercy's sake. And summer! Far too hot for such nonsense.

Bates was a short, round woman with an impressive head of iron-gray curls shoved up under a starched white cap. She wore a black dress—just as starched and stiff as the butler's collar—that looked like it had come from the last century. I wondered vaguely if our host liked his staff to play dress-up, or if these particular servants just preferred the old ways. At least they'd eschewed powdered wigs.

"Has my maid arrived?" I asked Bates's ramrod straight back.

"She arrived this morning, my lady. Along with your luggage. I believe she is currently unpacking."

Well, that was alright then. I'd been a little worried. Maddie was an excellent maid, if a little odd and a bit forthright. However, I'd never had the opportunity to travel with her, and sending her on ahead with both my and Aunt Butty's luggage—her own maid, Flora, being left behind in London—had made me a touch nervous.

Up the broad stairs—past portraits of grim ancestors—and to the right, a further turn left, and Bates left us in front of a door. "This will be your room, Lady Rample. Lady Lucas, yours is just across the hall. Dinner will be served at 8pm sharp." Her beady eyes latched onto me in an almost accusing manner. As if I'd ever been late for a meal in my life.

"I don't suppose you could manage to send up a pot of tea in the meantime," I said dryly. "Perhaps a bite to eat. My aunt and I have had quite the trip."

"Of course, my lady," Bates said grudgingly. And with that, she did a sharp one-eighty and bustled down the hall.

"Well, I never," Aunt Butty said with understandable outrage as the rustle of crinolines retreated.

"Maybe she doesn't care for guests."

"She's paid to care," Aunt Butty said stiffly. "Believe me, I shall bring this up with Harry."

Harry deVane being our host. Although lacking a title or any sort of pedigree, somehow the man had made an insane amount of money, purchased this manor house in Devon from an impoverished peer, and inserted himself into upper crust British society while still maintaining an edge of mystery and, dare I say, danger. He was just Aunt Butty's sort of person. Which, no doubt, was how she'd managed to wrangle an invite for both of us. Aunt Butty certainly had her ways.

Personally, I'd never met the man, but I'd been more than happy to leave London and my townhouse stewing in the summer heat while I escaped for a fortnight to the relative cool and fresh air of the country. Not to mention I'd heard rumors of Harry deVane's parties, and I'd been at something of a loss for good entertainment since my favorite jazz club had been shut down.

My dearest friend, Chaz, had tried desperately to introduce me to all sorts of hedonistic delights in the guise of music clubs and house parties, but none of them could rouse me from my funk. I refused to consider that it might not be lack of entertainment at all, but lack of one specific person who was probably swanning about France and had forgotten all about me.

Giving myself a stern internal order to quit messing about and get on with it, I pushed open the door to my room. It was lovely. One end of the room held a large, comfortable looking walnut-framed bed piled high with a rose-colored satin quilt and far too many pillows for one person. At the foot of the bed was a cozy, overstuffed armchair in violet blue. To the right was a chaise longue that matched the bed and an armoire, also walnut, from which a bony chintz-covered backside currently extended, and a rather tuneless humming emanated.

"Maddie?"

There was a squeak, and the backside disappeared to be replaced by a whole person. Maddie's narrow face was flushed from exertion and her hickory brown hair stuck up in several directions, having escaped the braids wrapped around her head like a milkmaid. She was a little thing, no more than twenty-five, with dark eyes far too shrewd for one so young. "M'lady. You've come." She sounded astonished as if she'd expected me to get lost somewhere on the road between London and Devon.

"Of course, I have. It's gone three." I calmly pulled off my gloves and handed them to her along with my handbag.

"Right." She turned and stuffed my possessions into the wardrobe. "'Course. Er, I haven't finished putting away for her ladyship."

"Lady Lucas?" I asked.

"Right. Lady Lucas." Maddie shot my aunt an apologetic look. "Sorry, your ladyship. I'll get to it soon as ever I can."

"No worries." Aunt Butty waved a beringed hand as she plopped down onto the chaise longue and arranged herself artfully as if posing for a painting. If the stories she told were true, this wouldn't be the first time she'd struck such a pose. Although this time she was likely wearing more clothing. "I shall rest here until you are finished. I feel in dire need of a rest."

In reality, she probably just didn't want to miss out on tea. Not that I blamed her. I was famished.

"I'll be finished in a tick," Maddie promised, turning back to the wardrobe.

"No rush," I assured her. Although what she'd been doing all this time, I'd no idea. I'd sent her down on the early morning train, so she should have arrived a good two hours ago. No doubt she'd been napping. Or reading one of the romance novels she'd filched from my library.

A few more trips back and forth to the pile of luggage near the door and she had stuffed everything in the wardrobe. The small vanity was already crammed with all my lotions and cosmetics. With a final nod she declared, "I shall have the footmen remove the luggage. I'll go unpack for Lady Butty."

"Lady Lucas," I corrected, but I was talking to the door.

"I swear, these girls never learn. Now fork over that flask. I know you have one." Aunt Butty gave me a knowing look.

With a sigh, I opened my handbag and pulled out a silver flask—another gift from my late husband, Lord Rample—which, naturally, contained whiskey. If anyone asked, I considered it medicinal. Which, without ginger ale, it was.

Aunty Butty took a deep swig and let out a sigh. "Much better. My nerves are overwrought. Your driving is enough to lead a nun to sin."

I eyed her askance as I took the flask back. "You exaggerate."

"Hardly." She scowled. "Whoever taught you to drive has a lot to answer for. Now where is that tea?"

"You'd think they'd have proper afternoon tea at a house party," I said. "This is quite a posh estate. Why aren't we being served in the drawing room? Or at least on the lawn?"

"DeVane is an Original. He does things on his own time and in his own way. He didn't get where he is by kowtowing to the masses."

"He'd do better to kowtow to his guests," I muttered as my stomach gave an unholy growl. I was beyond hungry and in desperate need of a cocktail.

I knew little of our host. He was a crony of Aunt Butty's, one of those sorts who, while having no title himself, was richer than God and somehow had half the peerage dancing to his tune. According to Butty, he'd acquired Wit's End some time ago, but had only recently finished fixing it up. This fortnight-long party was an excuse to show it off to a few friends and associates before throwing open the doors at the end of the party for a ball to impress the neighbors. As far as I was concerned, it was an excuse to get out of the blast furnace that was London in the summer.

I could have gone to my house in the south of France, of course. I'd yet to visit since Felix—Lord Rample—had shuffled off to the great poker game in the sky. But I'd been reluctant to leave the country, though I refused to admit it might have something to do with a certain musician who had wandered off to Paris a couple of months ago leaving me high and dry.

That wasn't entirely fair of me. Hale Davis was a working man and, once the Astoria Club in London closed, putting him out of a job, he had to go where the work was. I supposed I could have followed, but that seemed a little desperate. I am not the sort of woman to follow anyone.

There was the estate up north, of course. It had been entailed to one of Felix's cousins—along with the title. Unfortunately, the cousin, known as Bucktooth Binky to all and sundry, wasn't exactly speaking to me at the moment. He was rather sore over the fact that while he got a title and a great hulking monstrosity that was falling to ruin out in the wilds of Yorkshire, I got heaps and heaps of money, along with the London townhouse and the French villa. I suppose I could understand his petulance, but it meant I couldn't exactly drive up and ask to stay the summer.

"How did you meet this deVane person again?" I asked, digging through my handbag for a tin of fruit drops. It was nearly empty, but perhaps it would take the edge off my hunger. I popped one in my mouth and savored the sweet tart burst of lemon on my tongue.

"Oh, you know how it is," Aunt Butty said airily.

"A party?" I guessed.

"In Paris. What a marvelous time. The Belle Époque. So delicious." She sighed dramatically. "He was playing the piano—he does you know. Play that is. When it suits him, which it rarely does. Some woman or other was making a hash of singing along. Naturally I had to show her how to do it properly."

"Naturally," I said dryly. Aunt Butty was not one to stand in the shadows when she could do it better. And I don't mean that in a bad way. Aunt Butty couldn't help herself. She simply had to shine. She had too much charisma for her own good. "And did you and Mr. deVane, er…" How to put this tactfully?

"You want to know if we ever made whoopee?"

I almost choked on a boiled sweet. Leave it to Aunt Butty to get down to brass tacks. "Well, we are in the man's house and I want to know if there's going to be any awkwardness."

"There may have been some shenanigans back in the day, but we were young then. And possibly pickled. Now we are just good friends and Harry has varied and interesting tastes." But the sly look she gave me told me that while she may not be young anymore, she wasn't above getting pickled and getting Harry deVane into bed again.

There was a knock at the door, and a footman arrived with a laden tray which he thunked down on the small table beneath the window. Without a word, he stomped to the pile of empty luggage, scooped it up, and stomped out. The door swung shut with a bang behind him.

"Well, I *never*…" Aunt Butty blinked at the closed door.

"Perhaps you should talk to your Original friend about his Original servants," I said dryly as I inspected the tea service. At least the tea was properly brewed and there was plenty of cream and sugar. Though the two scanty biscuits were less than impressive. "If this tea is any indication of what we're going to be fed, I'm bound to waste away to nothing."

Which, while the current fashion, wasn't my natural state. I tended to be rather on the curvy side.

"Harry deVane and I have a lot to talk about." From Aunt Butty's tone, I had a feeling it wouldn't be pleasant for poor deVane.

I awoke at half seven that evening. Aunt Butty had gone off to her room after downing a cup of tea, leaving me to my own devices. Oppressive heat and an early morning had finally caught up with me and I'd nodded off at last, only to be woken by Maddie just in time to get myself together for dinner.

A good thing, too. I was hungry enough to storm the kitchen. Not the done thing at all.

With hair and makeup repaired, and dressed in a royal blue silk evening dress and a simple sapphire necklace, I exited my room and headed for the stairs. I got a bit turned around for a moment and ended up in some other wing of the manor. Instead of grim ancestors, there were rather bawdy paintings of lushly bottomed ladies lounging in ponds.

I had just turned around to retrace my steps when a door behind me opened. "Well, well. If it isn't the Merry Widow."

I turned around in surprise. I'd know that slurring voice anywhere. "Well, well," I echoed. "If it isn't Bucktooth Binky. What the devil are you doing here?"

Chapter 2

"I could ask you the same," Binky said sharply, stiffening at the detested nickname. There was certainly a reason for it. With his narrow and oversized teeth, he looked exactly like a rodent.

"I was invited," I said calmly.

"As was I." He gave me a bland, if slightly smug smile, smoothing back his mouse brown hair which was thinning rather alarmingly on top. He looked nothing like his cousin, who had still been quite handsome for a man in his sixties and with a full head of silver hair.

"I'm surprised you get invited anywhere."

His rat-like face flushed crimson. "You little trollop."

"Careful, Binky. Remember, I'm Felix's widow and I could buy and sell you ten times over." Rubbing his face in it probably wasn't the smartest thing, but I loathed him so. And, frankly, he deserved it. Calling me a trollop. He was one to talk.

If my late husband had one regret, it was that he had no proper heir to pass on the title. Instead, it would go to Alphonse Flanders—Bucktooth Binky—a distant cousin who'd been banking on the inheritance his entire life. Instead of doing anything useful, he'd spent that life in dissolution, partying and womanizing, getting himself into an atrocious amount of debt at gaming tables across Europe, and generally making a nuisance of himself. Felix had hated him, but there'd been nothing he could do. Except to leave his unentailed money and properties, which Binky had expected to inherit along with the entailed property, to me instead. The only thing Binky got was a drafty mansion in the middle of nowhere and a pile of debt he couldn't pay. I didn't feel the least bit sorry for him.

Binky's face flushed crimson, which clashed rather awfully with his claret colored double-breasted dinner jacket. He clearly wanted to say something—likely something off-colored and rude—but he managed to hold his tongue. Possibly because Aunt Butty took the opportunity to make her appearance.

We'd reached the head of the stairs when she came swanning down the hall. She wore a bronze lamé dinner dress that had a high square neck which entirely failed to hide her impressive bosom. She was sans hat, with her iron-gray hair neatly tucked in rolls and waves about her handsome face and pinned back with a gold hair pin shaped like a giant scarab beetle. She wore the most audacious orange topaz dangle earrings which matched the large, oval pin on her dress and the enormous cocktail ring she sported on her left hand.

"Ophelia, why ever are you dawdling on the stairs? We shall surely miss supper. Oh, hello, Binky." Her tone was cool, and her gaze passed over him, unimpressed.

Binky flushed a deeper crimson but remained silent. Which was well for him. Aunt Butty could have a barbed tongue when she wanted to. And she loathed the newest

Lord Rample with the heat of a thousand suns. My late husband had been a favorite of hers.

I bit back my amusement as we descended the stairs. Binky was used to people fawning over him. While he was a bit weak-chinned and wispy haired, he wasn't unhandsome. And with a title to his name, there were plenty of women willing to overlook his lack of funds. To have two women singularly unimpressed by his charms was enough to give him an apoplectic fit. The minute we hit the bottom of the stairs, he strode away without a backward glance.

My dearest friend, Charles Raynott, met us as we entered the drawing room. "Ladies, you look stunning."

"Chaz, darling, fancy seeing you here," I said, giving him a proper kiss on the cheek. Those ridiculous air kisses women of my station were so fond of giving were beyond me. "You're looking rather delicious yourself."

And he was. The man could give Clark Gable a run for his money. He was perfectly turned out in a black evening suit which set off his broad shoulders rather well and his hair had been brushed and oiled to perfection.

"Aunt Butty wrangled me an invitation at the last minute. Hello, ducks." He swooped to give her a hug. "Good thing, too. I was positively wasting away in that loathsome heat. You know I detest London in summer."

Aunt Butty patted his cheek. "Aren't you a doll. Now I must go and greet our host." She toddled off toward a tall, white haired gentleman who was dressed head to toe in black.

"Scrummy, isn't he?" Chaz murmured.

"If you like that sort."

"What's not to like? He's handsome, rich, and highly entertaining. Plus, his house isn't bad." He glanced around at the drawing room which was done in the height of modernist fashion with simple, curving lines and a great deal of glass and mirrors. The predominant color was lime green. Rather startling in large quantities, and out of place in the historical home. "Although it could use an expert touch."

"I thought you were off to the Continent," I said blandly, switching subjects. Recently. he'd met some French gentleman with more money than sense and had promptly disappeared, leaving me to my own devices.

Chaz waved languidly. "Old news, darling. He was too, too stuffy. And not nearly rich enough."

"Spun you a good story, did he?" Poor Chaz. Always falling for the wrong men.

"Dreadful liar. Should be shot."

I knew there was more to it, but he clearly didn't want to talk about it, so I didn't push. Instead, we wandered over to a brass and glass hostess cart which was loaded up with martini glasses filled with violet blue liquid and garnished with dark red maraschino cherries imported from Italy.

"Aviation cocktails, lovely!" Chaz exclaimed, claiming a glass for each of us. "I know it's got gin, darling, but do try it."

I was generally not a huge fan of gin, the highball being my poison of choice. But the sweet, floral chill of the creme de violette was astonishingly delicious. It tasted of sky and magic and summer nights. I downed mine rather too quickly and snagged a second. Divine. I made a mental note to send Maddie for the ingredients the minute we were back in London.

Aunt Butty beckoned and we were introduced to our host, the tall white-haired gentleman, Harry deVane. He insisted we call him Harry. I'd met him briefly when my Felix was alive. Some party or other, now a blur in my memory. He greeted us heartily and pressed Chaz's hand rather longer than necessary. I exchanged a knowing look with Aunt Butty. Apparently, Harry deVane appreciated beauty regardless of form.

"I do apologize about Binky," he said in a warm, rumbly voice. "Business, you know. I simply had to invite him. I hadn't realized..."

"I told him about our Binky issues," Aunt Butty said. "The little pipsqueak better be on his best behavior."

"No worries," I assured Harry. "I have no issues with him other than his attitude."

Harry seemed surprised at my bluntness, then laughed. "Refreshing. I do love a woman who speaks her mind."

No wonder he adored my aunt. The woman had elevated speaking her mind to an art form.

"Nice little gathering you've got here, Harry," Chaz said, taking a sip of his violet drink and edging closer to our handsome host.

"Isn't it, though? You know Bucktooth Binky, of course." Harry smirked. "What a delightful nickname. I must remember to use it. The couple hovering by the drinks cart is Maude and Mathew Breverman. Met them on a cruise down the Nile. Interesting couple. American. He's in textiles. Worth more than I am. Can you believe? Trying to convince me to go into business with him."

Maude was a plump, middle-aged woman with frightfully frizzy blonde hair done up in a semblance of the current fashion. Unfortunately, it wouldn't stay put and ended up looking like cotton wool stuck on her head. Mathew was equally plump and looked a veritable penguin in his black tuxedo. He had a thin moustache dusting his upper lip, and squinty little eyes that were altogether too shrewd.

"Who are the two women near the fire?" I asked.

The first woman, tall and spare with a long, horse-like face, appeared to be in, perhaps, her fifties. The second, short and plump with quick, bird-like movements and large cow eyes, was somewhat younger. They were both dressed in evening gowns that were at least fifteen or twenty years out of date with loose waists and an inordinate number of ruffles. The persimmon and rose-colored fabrics clashed wildly with the room's décor and their wearers' complexions.

"Those are the Sisters Kettington," Harry explained. "The tall one is Ethel, and the other, Amelia. Neighbors of mine. Their family was once quite wealthy but has since fallen on hard times. Very proper sorts of ladies. I thought they might enjoy some time away from their little cottage."

That was kind of him. I hadn't expected a man like Harry to think of his impoverished neighbors, even if they were proper sorts.

"The woman lounging on the divan is one Miss Semple," Harry continued. "She's been after me for yonks. Father is some kind of landed gentry. You can imagine what she's after."

The woman was about my age—middle thirties—with neatly waved dark hair, carefully penciled arched brows, and perfectly painted coral lips. Her skin was milk white and there was plenty of it on display thanks to her backless, sleeveless green silk gown. She caught us staring and fluttered her ridiculously oversized lashes. I was fairly certain they were fake.

"Why did you invite her if she's such a trial?" Aunt Butty asked.

Harry chuckled. "It amused me."

My estimation of Harry went down a notch. He had no intention of being ensnared by Miss Semple, but he was fine toying with her. Like a cat with a mouse. It was a most unattractive quality.

"What an odd assortment of people," Chaz mused, sipping his cocktail.

"Aren't they just," Harry agreed. "I think it's terribly dull having the same sort of people around all the time, don't you? In fact, we'll have a few extras at dinner tonight. The more the merrier, eh?"

At that moment, the door swung open and in walked Lord Peter Varant. My heart gave an irrational flutter as he turned to me and a small smile pulled at his handsome, saturnine features. He was impeccably turned out. Thick, chestnut hair swept back from a high forehead and high cheekbones. Every inch of him perfectly manicured.

"Well, look who the cat dragged in," Chaz muttered. "Do I need to protect your honor?"

I ignored him. Sometimes it was the only thing one could do. I hadn't seen Varant since the shenanigans at the Astoria Club a few months ago. Oh, sure, we'd tried to get together a couple of times, but it never seemed to work out. He was either being called away by some issue on one of his properties or dashing off to attend to some matter of state—he did something with the government, though I wasn't sure what. It was all terribly hush hush. Meanwhile I had been trying to make up for lost time after Felix's death. The never-ending whirlwind of parties and dinners and galas had left me exhausted. This holiday was a welcome one.

It didn't surprise me that Varant knew Harry. Varant knew pretty much everyone. It did surprise me a little to see him at this party. I hadn't expected it. It didn't seem his type of thing. Then again, I wasn't sure what his type of thing was. Though I'd been acquainted with him for awhile now, since before Felix died, I really didn't know him that well. He liked to play things close to the vest.

"By jove. Look who's with Varant," Chaz muttered.

The man was slender, gray haired, with a bristly moustache. He looked vaguely familiar, but I couldn't place him.

"It's the Chancellor of the Exchequer, Neville Chamberlain. What's he doing here? It's not exactly his scene." Chaz frowned. "Isn't he supposed to be busy putting the economy back together?"

Harry strode toward the newcomers, arms outstretched. "Neville, old bean!"

The two men shook each other's hands and did that back patting thing that men do. Harry greeted Varant the same way, though Varant was less enthusiastic about it than Chamberlain had been.

"Harry was at Mason College with Chamberlain," Aunt Butty confided. "I think he issued an invitation to our little soiree in hopes the two of them could speak about business matters. Harry has interests in several foreign companies."

I frowned. "Why would our host want to speak to Chamberlain? It's not like he's going to change the man's mind about tariffs and import duties."

"No, but he likely thinks he can convince Chamberlain to give him special consideration," Chaz said. "I doubt it will work what with the debt repayment to America. And then there's the German issue. That could go wonky."

"German issue?" I asked.

"Hitler," Aunt Butty said dryly, polishing off her cocktail. "Harry is not thrilled about the situation."

"You mean that smug little man in Germany?" I asked.

"The same."

"But he lost the election," I pointed out.

"Still, his party won a lot of power. There are those who feel Hitler is dangerous and they are very concerned. Chamberlain doesn't think so. He believes he can handle Hitler. Very short-sighted if you ask me." Aunt Butty's entire body quivered with outrage. "The man is an undeniable racist."

"Chamberlain?" I asked.

"No. Well, I don't know. But I meant Hitler. Insufferable man." Aunt Butty liberated another drink from the hostess cart and downed it in one go. "I read that dreadful book of his. Appalling. Filled with racist nonsense. Mark my words, no good will come of this!"

Just then, Jarvis appeared and rang the gong for dinner. We all filed into the dining room, which was decorated like a medieval banquet hall. The walls were plastered stone, the floors flagstone, the table a massive oak monstrosity, and the chairs upholstered in red velvet. In one corner stood an actual suit of armor complete with broadsword. Colorful pendants hung from the ceiling, and there was a fireplace large enough to roast an entire cow.

"Ghastly," Aunt Butty whispered. "And I thought the drawing room was bad. The man has no sense of taste."

Which was rather rich coming from a woman who wore entire birds on her head. I wish I were joking, but alas, I am not. Aunt Butty had the most atrocious taste in hats.

We were all seated around the table, Harry at the head with Chamberlain on his right and Aunt Butty—being the oldest and the highest-ranking woman—at the foot acting as hostess. Which tickled her no end. She forgave Harry his taste in decor immediately.

I was seated across from Chaz and between Mathew Breverman and Miss Semple. I would have preferred to be seated next to Chaz or Varant. Better yet, both. I could flirt with Varant and snark with Chaz about the other guests.

Over a first course of celery soup, I turned to Mathew Breverman. "I understand you and your wife met our host on a Nile cruise. That sounds rather exciting. I've never been to Egypt."

"Frightful place. Hot as hell and flies everywhere. But Harry is a good guy. We played poker. Won a buck or two off him." He chuckled. "Not a bad, player, though."

Then I made the mistake of asking him about his work in textiles.

His eyes lit up immediately. "No one understands how dam—er, doggone hard it is in textiles these days, Lady R."

I winced at the familiarity. "Lady Rample." I wasn't one to care much for formality or proper titles. I'd been raised a vicar's daughter, after all. But Breverman was one of those sorts that one had to stand up to or be plowed under.

He barreled on, ignoring me. So much for standing. "It's a rough job these days, what with the newfangled machines and the price of cotton. Not to mention that Chamberlain fellow trying to weasel out of the debts you people owe from the Great War."

You people? Had he really just said that? I had a good mind to stab him in the leg with my fork. He didn't notice my rising ire but rambled on. I tuned him out, occasionally smiling and nodding. I simply couldn't embarrass Aunt Butty by getting blood all over Harry's white tablecloth. Though she would definitely have understood. Even applauded.

Every now and then I caught Varant glancing my way from up the table. His expression was unreadable, but was that a smolder in his eye? It was hard to say, but I liked to think it was.

Over the main dish—savory roast chicken in rich cream with noodles and fresh green vegetables—I was finally able to turn to Miss Semple. I found her a more entertaining dinner companion.

She amused me with tales of herself and her older sister. "No boys, you see. Father was most disappointed. All that cost coming out and Annabella only managed to bag a mere Mister. Did you have a coming out, Lady Rample?"

"Of a sort." Aunt Butty, after rescuing me from being locked in my room and having my sins prayed over, had whisked me off to London. She hadn't bothered with any of that coming out nonsense. "*Waste of time and money*," she used to say. Instead she introduced me to interesting people, regardless of rank or wealth. "But I was a bit of an old maid when I married."

She laughed. "That's what my father calls me. Says I'm nothing but an expense." She eyed Harry deVane. "I'll show him."

I had no doubt that Miss Semple was a determined young woman, but she was barking up the wrong tree there. I did, however, hope she did show her father one way or another. I knew what it was like having an overbearing father.

We finished off the meal with paradise pudding dripping with fresh berries followed by a cheese plate. I managed to avoid further conversation with Mathew Breverman by the sheer fact that Ethel Kettington monopolized his time. She should know better, but I wasn't offended. In fact, I was relieved.

When I wasn't speaking with Miss Semple, I snuck glances down the table at Varant who now barely seemed to notice me. I was a bit put out. After all, on previous meetings he'd behaved as if he had some interest of the romantic variety. In fact, earlier this evening he'd been all smoldering glances, and here he was acting as if I didn't exist!

At last dinner was over and the women retreated to the drawing room while the men remained at table to puff on their smelly cigars, drink port, and ramble about politics. Meanwhile, we women were to sit and gossip politely over coffee. Which I found unutterably dull.

Once again, Ethel dominated the conversation. "This used to be our home once, didn't it Amelia? Yes, we grew up here," she barreled on without waiting for her sister to answer. "The décor was more tasteful, of course. My mother had exquisite taste."

"Did Mr. deVane buy it from you?" Maude Breverman asked somewhat gauchely.

Ethel stiffened. "Indeed not. My father sold the manor many years ago to another gentleman. We don't mind. We much prefer our little cottage. Very comfortable." She droned on, but I had tuned her out.

As soon as it was possible to excuse myself, I slipped out of the drawing room, ostensibly to powder my nose. In reality, I just wanted away from the inanity.

I decided a walk outside and a bit of fresh air would do me some good, so I wandered toward the nearest exit. As I passed the dining room, I noticed the door was open a crack and men's voices rumbled through the hall. I paused a moment, curious. What did men talk about when we ladies weren't present?

Quietly as possible, I tiptoed toward the open door, pausing just out of sight. Mostly it was boring political talk, as I suspected. But just as I gave up and started to move down the hall, one word caught my attention.

"—spies."

I froze. Spies? Here in Devon? Surely not. Who would spy down here? And on what? Or whom?

Indistinct male voices made sounds of protestation.

"I know you find it hard to believe, Neville," Harry boomed, "but I assure you, there's no doubt of it."

"I simply cannot fathom it, Harry." I assumed that was Neville Chamberlain answering. "It just isn't..." The rest of his words were indistinguishable.

I listened a bit longer, but nothing else of interest was said. The sound of wood scraping on stone jarred me.

Then came Harry's voice again. "Gentlemen, shall we join the ladies?"

Hurrying as quickly as I could, I darted around a corner before one of the men could catch me eavesdropping. My mind was a whirl, curiosity driving me to near madness. A spy. How curious. If only I knew what all this was about.

I determined to ask Chaz the moment I could get him alone.

Chapter 3

The evening passed in a haze of nervous energy. I could focus on nothing else save getting Chaz alone and putting the screws to him—as they say in American films.

After the gentlemen rejoined us, the Brevermans and Kettingtons sat down for a few hands of cards, proceeding to ignore the rest of the party. Chaz pawed through Harry's record collection, finally selecting "Mad About the Boy" while Miss Semple flirted with him madly, to no avail. Harry secreted himself away in his office with Chamberlain and Varant. And Binky pouted in a corner, as was typical of Binky.

Aunt Butty had begged off and gone to her room, claiming exhaustion from the journey. I knew it was nonsense, of course. Aunt Butty had more energy than the lot of us put together. What she had was the latest Agatha Christie which I'd loaned her after reading it myself. I'd also seen her liberate a bottle of port from the liquor cabinet, so I'd no doubt she was in for a pleasant evening.

I lounged in a chair by the window, which was open to let in the cool evening breeze. A pleasant change from the heavy, hot London air. There was the scent of fresh green things, the heady perfume of roses, and the call of a night bird. I'd be tempted to buy my own country home if it weren't for the lack of civilization.

My mind drifted to Varant, secreted away in Harry's office. I hadn't had a chance for more than a passing greeting, and it left me frustrated. Aunt Butty was certain he was interested in me, but he played so hot and cold. What did it mean? Did I even care?

Then I caught movement out of the corner of my eye, startling me from my reverie. I stared hard out into the darkness. Had I been imagining things? No, there it was again. Just beyond the window, someone moving in the bushes. I leaned forward eagerly, practically sticking my head outside to get a better look. A dark figure—definitely a man, with a slight stoop to his shoulders and the distinctive outline of a bowler hat—moved swiftly through the garden, disappearing into the trees at the far edge of the grounds in the direction of the village. I frowned. Maybe it was just one of the servants slipping off to the pub. Then again—

Chaz slumped into the chair next to me, shattering my concentration. He'd somehow made his escape from Miss Semple. "Lord, this is a tedious group, don't you think? Not nearly as glamorous as I'd hoped." He dangled a champagne glass from one hand—no idea where he'd got the stuff—and stared morosely out the window into the dark. "But free booze, I suppose, if nothing else. And the food was delicious. As is our host. If he'd ever come out of his study."

"Your conversation earlier seemed quite interesting," I said.

He frowned. “That ghastly woman rambling about her Siamese? Thank goodness she didn’t bring it here. Can you imagine?”

“People don’t usually bring cats to house parties,” I said drily.

“Small miracle.”

“But I wasn’t talking about your tête-à-tête with Miss Semple. I was speaking of the conversation you gentlemen were having over port and cigars. I heard someone mention a spy.”

His eyebrows lifted. “Oh, that. Wasn’t paying much attention, darling. Beverman was droning on about…good gosh, I don’t even know. Likely Harry was asking Neville Chamberlain about the German situation.”

“I didn’t know we had a German situation.” Neville Chamberlain, being Chancellor of the Exchequer, was certainly more in the know about such things than I.

“We don’t. Yet. But there are some—including Harry—who are convinced that things are about to go amok what with Hitler’s party gaining power and denying the Treaty of Versailles and all that. Chamberlain and his ilk consider that an exaggeration and think that those like Harry are seeing spies where there are none. That sort of thing.”

“Why would Germany spy on England?” I asked.

He gave me a look. “They did in during the war, you know.”

“I’m not an idiot. Of course I know. But we are not at war. Why would they send spies now?”

"Why would anyone? The Americans do it all the time. Spy on everybody. Very suspicious, those Americans."

"But why Germany specifically?"

"Sherry, love?" At my nod, Chaz got up to refill my glass and get a sherry for himself, then sat back down. "Harry believes this Hitler bloke is up to no good. From what I've heard, he's probably not wrong. The man is certifiable. He wants Europe to give Germany back some of the territory they were forced to give up after losing the Great War. But our government thinks it can all be worked out peacefully. That it's only a small faction of the German citizenry that approves of Hitler and his followers. So, it'll come to nothing. But Harry thinks he—Hitler, that is—is putting pieces in place for more nefarious purposes."

"Spies."

Chaz nodded. "I know it sounds mad. I mean, he lost the presidential election, but stranger things, don't you know. Still, I don't know that it will ever happen again. Not a war like that. Surely everyone has learned their lesson and things can be worked out in a more civilized manner."

It did sound concerning. Still...spies? In Devon? "So, they were talking about Germany, then?"

"I assume so. If you heard them talking about spies, but like I said, I wasn't paying attention."

"Wait," I said, glass halfway to my lips as a thought struck. "Do you suppose Harry thinks spies are here in Devon because Chamberlain is here in Devon?"

"Likely."

"Why *is* Chamberlain in Devon?"

Chaz gave me a knowing look and took a sip of sherry. "Both Chamberlain and Harry claim they're just old friends catching up but come now. Chamberlain isn't staying for the party and he came with Varant. You know he does...whatever he does for the government."

I nodded. It was known in a vague sort of way that Lord Varant did *something* for the government. What that something was, well, that was a matter of wild speculation because no one actually knew except Varant himself. And he wasn't talking. Aunt Butty was half convinced he was the next Scarlet Pimpernel.

"And see how Harry deserted his guests to secrete himself away with two government men? Well, what do you think that means?" Chaz asked.

"They're up to something."

"No doubt."

We sipped our sherries in silence.

"I can almost hear your brain working from here," Chaz murmured.

"You know curiosity is my greatest weakness."

"Good lord, tell me you're not going to play detective again," he said.

"Fine, then. I won't," I said smugly.

Chaz groaned.

I almost told him about the figure in the garden. The spy perhaps? But I decided to keep it to myself. For now. Just in case it was nothing.

The next morning dawned far too bright for my taste. The curtain fabric was lovely, but too lightweight to keep out the morning sun. Plus, Maddie marched in with tea far before I was ready to rise.

"Too early," I mumbled, burrowing under the duvet. It smelled of lilac water and sunshine.

"Nonsense," Maddie said. "It's gone ten. If you don't get down to breakfast, there'll be nothing left. That Binky person is on his third plate." I could almost hear the disapproving scowl in her voice.

I lifted the duvet so I could stare at her with one bleary eye. "However do you know that?"

"Vera told me. She's one of the upstairs maids." She set the tea on the side table with an almighty rattle. "She doesn't like that Binky person any more than I do."

"Oh." I pulled the duvet back over my head. "And he's Lord Rample to you."

She snorted. "Never. Your husband—God rest his soul—was the true Lord Rample. That upstart can never take his place."

I probably should have reprimanded her, but I hadn't the heart to. It amused me that she referred to Felix's relation as an upstart, and I despised Binky nearly as much as she did.

"Tea m'lady." Maddie shoved a cup beneath my nose. Clearly, she was familiar with what it took to get me out of bed.

I managed a seated position while she plumped the pillows behind me. The first sip was sweet, dark heaven and cleared the muzzy cobwebs from my mind.

"Spies!"

Maddie blinked, hand hovering over the wardrobe door knob. "Wot's that, m'lady?"

"Last night," I said, leaning forward so eagerly I nearly sloshed tea on myself, "I overheard the men talking. They said there's a spy in our midst."

"A spy, m'lady?" She blinked owlishly.

I nodded. "Yes." I took another fortifying sip of tea.

"What sort of spy?"

"A German one."

She frowned, and I noticed her hand shook a little as she grasped the wardrobe knob and flung open the door. "Nonsense. Why would a German spy be in Devon? What would they spy on?"

"My thought exactly. I'm going to find out!"

She whirled, face pale. "No!"

I lifted a brow. "Excuse me?"

She blanched further. "N-no, m'lady. You should leave that sort of thing to the experts wot know wot they're doing. It's not safe."

"This is Devon, as you so rightly pointed out. I doubt anything terrible will happen. I bet I can find the spy before anyone else. How hard can it be?"

She shook her head, eyes wide. "M'lady! You mustn't!"

"Maddie—"

She stomped her foot. "The Huns are dastardly, m'lady. Beware!"

Chapter 4

Maddie had refused to say anything more and had instead stormed out of my room without so much as offering to help with my hair. Not that I needed help. I'd been raised without much in the way of money, and certainly without a maid, so I was used to doing for myself. Still, it was annoying. I'd have to have a word with her later.

I was also concerned. Why was she so worried about my being in danger? The idea of German spies seemed to terrify her more than was normal. I supposed it could have something to do with her background…

Something I'd have to suss out later. With a mental shrug, I set it all aside for now and finished both my tea and my toilette. After donning a simple blue cotton day dress, I fluffed my hair and swiped on some raspberry red lipstick before descending to breakfast.

"Have you heard the news?" Aunt Butty accosted me as I entered the dining room, following the aroma of bacon and toast. We were the only two in the room. Either the others had already eaten and were out and about, or the rest of the party were even later risers than I was.

"What news?" I asked as I helped myself from the still steaming silver chafing dishes on the antique mahogany sideboard. In addition to fried eggs and bacon, there was a large dish of kedgeree, which I avoided, toast, and a pot of marmalade. There was also a large urn of coffee to which I helped myself. Liberally.

"We were robbed last night."

I nearly dropped the serving fork into the bacon. "What?"

"Harry's study was ransacked," Aunt Butty said with no little glee. "He found it this morning and went on an absolute tear. You should have seen it!"

"I thought Harry was your friend," I chided.

"He is," she said mildly. "Doesn't mean I don't enjoy a little drama now and then."

Which was true. Aunt Butty was the Queen of Drama.

A fact which was borne out in her current ensemble. She wore a one-piece pant-suit sort of thing with a crisscrossed bodice and wide, flowing trousers. The fabric was puce with dark plum swirls over it. Over the top of the pantsuit she wore a lightweight, mustard yellow kimono-style cardigan and around her neck a cotton scarf of sky blue the same color as my dress. She wore no hat, but I'd no doubt there was one just waiting in the wings. The outfit was...eye catching, to say the least.

"Was anything stolen?" I asked, adding a couple of eggs to my plate.

"No idea. I haven't been able to get him aside to ask." She gave a huff of frustration.

"Did he call the police?"

She nodded, snagging a piece of toast and slathering it with butter and marmalade. "Naturally. He spent a good ten minutes shouting at the poor desk sergeant. They're sending someone around."

Though not in a hurry apparently. I wondered if I could get in and have a look around the office before the police arrived. I couldn't help but think this may have something to do with the spy.

"Aunt Butty," I said as we sat at the table, "I overheard something last night." I gave her a quick rundown of what I'd heard while the men were at port, what I'd seen in the garden, and my conversations later with Chaz and Maddie.

"A spy in our midst? And a German at that. How thrilling!" Aunt Butty didn't seem at all phased, which was no surprise. She took a sip of coffee. "Do you suppose it was this spy who broke into the house and ransacked Harry's study? I'll bet he's the same person you saw skulking about the gardens!"

"It makes sense," I said. "Given that Harry met with Varant and Chamberlain in there last night. But Harry isn't with the government, is he?"

"Not at all. He's retired mostly, though he still owns several businesses. Manufacturing or some such thing. He's a philanthropist of the arts. Nothing governmental about it. But that Chamberlain was here along with Varant. Maybe his visit got this spy person in a twist." She glanced about as if the spy could be hiding behind the drapes. "Do you suppose the spy is here? In this house?"

"I doubt it. Not if he—or she—had to break in."

"Well, I don't know if anyone broke into the house. Just that they broke into the study. Harry keeps it locked when he's not using it."

Which was interesting. I wondered if that were usual, or if it was just because there were a lot of people staying in his house. Or, perhaps, if there was something special in his study that he needed to keep secured. So many possibilities that my brain itched with them.

Just then I heard male voices rumbling in the hall. I darted from my seat to the door to peek out. Sure enough, there was a uniformed policeman and with him, a man in a cheap brown suit. Most likely a detective. They were conversing with our host.

"Who is it?" Aunt Butty hissed from behind me.

I beckoned her to be quiet. "The police are here."

Which was too bad. Now I'd have to wait for them to leave before I could poke around the study. Although this did provide the perfect opportunity for eavesdropping.

"Was anything taken?" the man in the brown suit was asking Harry.

"It's hard to say." Was it just me, or was Harry hedging? "The place is an unholy mess."

"Any sign of break-in?"

"One of the French doors from the study to the terrace was smashed. Going to be an utter nightmare to replace." Harry sounded more irritated by the inconvenience than anything.

"So someone from the outside then," Brown Suit mused.

Which was wild speculation as far as I was concerned. Someone from the inside could have as easily set the scene to mislead the investigation.

"Anything of value missing?" Brown Suit asked.

"I don't know, do I? I called as soon as I saw the mess." Harry's voice held steady, but... I don't know. I just wasn't buying it. Not after the spy conversation and Chamberlain's visit. The three of them locked in that room. Now this?

"Let's have a look at it," Brown Suit said.

As their footsteps retreated down the hall, I pushed open the door further. "Come on," I hissed to Aunt Butty. "Let's see if we can hear anything more."

Leaving our half-eaten breakfasts, the two of us tiptoed down the hall in the direction of the study. The men had disappeared, and the study door now stood open. More rumbling voices could be heard inside.

Unfortunately, there was nowhere obvious for us to eavesdrop without running the risk of getting caught. No giant, potted plants. No drapes. No suits of armor to hide behind.

However, across from the study, and slightly closer to us, was another door. I wasn't sure where it led, but perhaps it would be a good place to duck into. If we left the door open a crack, we'd be able to hear what was said in the study.

We approached with caution and I pushed open the door. It opened onto a set of steps leading down, no doubt into the cellar. It was dark, dusty, and held a distinctly damp smell. With a shrug, I urged Aunt Butty through and stepped in behind her, pulling the door so that it was open just a crack.

We both squeezed together on the top step, ears pressed to the crack.

"…a key?" Brown Suit's voice rumbled down the hall.

"No. Just myself and my butler. No one else." Harry's voice held a tone of finality.

Brown Suit harrumphed, mumbled something—no doubt to his uniformed companion—and then said, "We can dust for prints."

"No. No. Not necessary. Nothing of import stolen, so no point." Was Harry lying? Why did he want to get rid of the police so quickly? Why call them if he didn't want them investigating?

Brown Suit must have been thinking along the same lines. "Mr. deVane, the police frown upon time wasters." I was certain if Harry had been anyone else—someone not filthy rich, for instance—Brown Suit would have had a few stronger words for him.

"Sorry there, detective—"

"Detective Inspector."

"Right. Well, you see, it was my butler that called. If I'd realized, I'd have stopped him. Sorry to waste your time. Would you like a coffee on your way out?"

"No thank you," Brown Suit said. His voice held a faint tremble of anger which he managed to restrain.

Footsteps echoed in the hall. Passed our hiding place. Hesitated.

"What the blazes is the cellar door doing open?" Harry said.

Before I could move, the door slammed shut and we were plunged into darkness.

"Get us out of here, Ophelia," Aunt Butty commanded. "I'm almost certain I've got spiders on me." She jiggled a bit as though trying to dislodge something, causing her rather impressive bosom to heave about in an undignified manner. I managed to repress a giggle, though my skin crawled at the thought of spiders.

I tried the door, but it was locked. "Er, Aunt Butty, I don't think we can get out."

"Don't be ridiculous. Just turn the knob."

"I can't. It's locked."

"Well, isn't this a fine kettle of fish," she snipped. "Now what do you propose? Beating on the door and screaming like a common workman?"

"Hardly," I said drily. "We don't exactly want Harry knowing we're sneaking around his house, do we?"

"Fair point."

"Surely there's a light. Feel around and see if you can find it."

We proceeded to pat the walls, feeling for switches. When that failed, we batted in the air like house cats, looking for a chain. No doubt we'd have looked ridiculous if there'd been anyone to see us. And if it hadn't been pitch-black.

Finally, Aunt Butty let out a crow of triumph. It was followed by a clicking sound, and then the stairwell filled with light from the bare bulb overhead.

"Well, that's a relief," Aunt Butty said. "Can you pick the lock?"

"Maybe." Chaz had taught me the trick one day when we were bored. And I'd had a chance to use it a time or two during my last investigation at the now defunct Astoria Club. I pulled a hair pin from my coiffure and knelt on the top step. It was difficult to see, since my body cast shadow over the lock, but I did my best.

Fifteen minutes later I realized the lock was beyond me. I sat down next to Aunt Butty, feeling grimy and damp with sweat, my fingers aching from the fine work. "This isn't going to work."

She sighed. "Then I suppose we must find another way out."

"From a cellar?"

"All these old houses have secret passageways and whatnot. There must be a back door at the very least," she said with confidence. Confidence I wasn't feeling.

We made our way cautiously down the old stone steps, worn and uneven from generations of feet. The floor was lined with flagstone, also uneven, but better than bare dirt, I suppose.

Aunt Butty propped her hands on her ample hips and turned slowly in circles. We were standing in the wine cellar. Four walls lined with wine racks, at least half of them filled with neatly labeled bottles. It was immaculately clean and free of dust.

"Jarvis must spend an inordinate amount of time down here," Aunt Butty muttered.

I didn't doubt that. In the center of the room was a plain wooden table next to which stood a matching chair with scuffed legs. On the table sat a wine bottle, neatly corked, but with half its contents gone. Next to it lay a twin-pronged cork puller.

"I think Jarvis may be sampling the wine," I said dryly. The butler's cork puller would allow him to remove the cork, drink the wine, replace it with cheaper stuff—or water it down—and replace the cork, all without damage. Harry would never know his wine had been tampered with unless he had a stellar palate.

"Stealing from his employer? That stiff?" Aunt Butty practically crowed. I'd no doubt that the minute we got out of here, she'd tell Harry. Or, more likely, use the threat of telling Harry to her advantage.

"I don't see another door," I said. Every wall was covered in wine racks.

"Nonsense. Haven't you heard of hidden doors?" Aunt Butty stepped to the nearest rack and gave it a pull. "Come on. Try it."

With a shrug, I started on the opposite side, and we worked our way toward each other. I was almost to the middle when a tug on the rack moved it an inch outward. "I think I found something."

She hurried over, and I gave a good pull on the rack. Once it was started, it swung easily, revealing a tunnel leading...I'd no idea where. But I could feel the faint flutter of air on my face. It smelled of damp earth, but it had to come from somewhere.

"There must be an exit down there," Aunt Butty confirmed my musings.

"We've no light," I said. "We'll have to do this in the dark." I wasn't thrilled with the idea.

"Buck up. We are women. Not mice." Aunt Butty marched ahead into the tunnel.

The walls had been whitewashed at one point, though the wash was now dirty and chipping. Cobwebs festooned the ceiling and draped elegantly down to brush our heads and shoulders. I shuddered at the skitter of tiny feet. This was not the sort of adventure I enjoyed.

After a brief discussion, we'd left the entrance open, so we could have at least a little light. We decided that while it would tip off the butler to invaders, he'd have no idea who the invaders were, or why they'd entered his domain. At least, not until Aunt Butty confronted him at the time and place of her choosing.

I nearly jumped out of my shoes when Aunt Butty let out a screech. I whirled to face her, half expecting to find her covered in spiders, or with a knife at her throat. But she just stood there looking terrified.

"What is it?"

"A ghost."

I blinked. "Pardon?"

"I am certain this place is haunted, Ophelia."

This was the downside of having a vivid imagination. "Nonsense. There are no such things as ghosts." At least, I hoped not.

She set her jaw. "Don't be so close-minded, niece. I am positive there's a ghost in here. I *felt* it."

I decided to humor her. "Fine. What did you feel?"

"It got very cold, and then something brushed my arm."

"It's cold because we're underground. And you probably brushed up against a spider web. There's a giant one dangling over there." I pointed to a thick swath of white webbing just behind her.

Aunt Butty let out a horrified gasp, snapped her mouth shut, and marched briskly down the tunnel ahead of me. I grinned. I supposed in the battle between fear of ghosts and fear of spiders, the spiders won.

The light grew dimmer as we moved further into the tunnel, but the air became fresher—less of damp earth and more of greenery and flowers—and the breeze teased at my hair. Eventually, the tunnel ahead of us turned from pitch black to gloomy gray. We must be nearing the exit.

Finally, we came across an iron-bound wood door that looked a few hundred years old at the least. There were large gaps at the top and bottom which allowed wind and light down the tunnel. I tested the handle to find that while the door was latched from the inside, it wasn't locked. I gave it a good push and it creaked open a foot or so before it stuck fast against the uneven ground.

"There's no way I'm getting through that tiny space," Aunt Butty said.

I rolled my eyes and squeezed myself into the gap. Using my body weight, I shoved at the door, managing to get it open a few more inches, just enough for both of us to squeeze through.

From the outside, the door was all but invisible, covered in thick, hanging ivy. There was no handle on this side, which meant there was no way for anyone to open it unless someone from the inside let them in. Hence it being unlocked.

"Well, that was an adventure," Aunt Butty said, shaking her clothes to rid them of dust and creatures. Her gray hair was festooned with cobwebs. I imagined mine fared no better.

"Good lord, what have the two of you been up to?"

We whirled to find Chaz staring at us, a smirk on his face, hands tucked in the pockets of his seersucker trousers. His matching suit coat was open to reveal a light blue cotton button up, open at the throat. It was too hot for a tie. A straw boater with a wide blue and red band was tipped at a rakish angle over his forehead.

"Um, we got lost," I said.

He smirked. "Liar. You were poking your nose where it didn't belong, weren't you?"

Might as well admit it. "Naturally."

"We were eavesdropping on the police," Aunt Butty explained calmly, "and got ourselves locked in the cellar."

"Why didn't you pick the lock?" Chaz asked, amused.

"I tried. I couldn't get it open. So we had to find another way out."

"A rather grubby one, by the looks of it." He reached out and flicked something from my shoulder.

"What was that?" I demanded suspiciously.

"Nothing." He gave an innocent little bat of his ridiculously thick lashes. I was so envious of those lashes. I had to wield my cake of mascara quite liberally to achieve the same effect. "I think the two of you might want to sneak in the back way and make some repairs. The police are questioning everyone, and your—ah—current appearance might be cause for suspicion."

He wasn't wrong there. "I thought Harry had convinced that detective person to leave."

"Apparently not. He's poking about, causing an uproar. Now get along with you before someone catches you."

"Promise you won't tell anyone?" I begged.

"Darling. As if you had to ask."

As Aunt Butty and I scurried toward our rooms, I could swear I heard him laughing at us.

Chapter 5

Aunt Butty and I managed to avoid the police and sneak upstairs to refresh ourselves. Maddie was nowhere to be seen, but once again, I didn't mind. No doubt she was pressing something. Or hiding in a corner with a book and a cup of tea, which she sometimes did when we were at home. It gave me the chance to clean up without her asking uncomfortable questions.

My clothes were a disaster, smeared with streaks of dirty gray, so I gave them a shake out the window to lose any creepy crawlies and draped them over the chaise longue. Maddie could have them washed later.

After repairing my makeup and fluffing my hair, ridding it of dust and cobwebs, I dug in my wardrobe for a new outfit. It was already getting rather warm, so I went with high-waisted, white trousers and a V-necked ribbed top that was navy and white striped. It was all very nautical. I tied a contrasting pink and white silk scarf around my throat, despite the heat. It was just too cute not to. I slipped on my white ghillies sandals with the red trim, tying them neatly around my trim ankles. I may have more curves than fashionable, but I was very proud of my ankles.

Looking rather more put together, I descended the stairs, only to be immediately caught out by Brown Suit.

"Ah ha!" He pointed a thick finger at me in an accusing manner.

"Ah ha, indeed. Do you mind pointing that thing elsewhere?" I drawled, continuing my leisurely downward decent, shooting him one of my languid lady-of-the-manor looks complete with nose in the air. Felix said I'd perfected it. I like to think so.

"Don't be a cad, Willis. This is Ophelia, Lady Rample, widow of the late Lord Rample. She's one of my houseguests." Harry appeared in a nearby doorway looking amused. Clearly, he wasn't taking the break-in, or this Willis person, seriously.

"Pardon me, your ladyship." Willis sketched an awkward bow, equal parts fawning and resentful. How he pulled that off, I couldn't imagine. "Detective Inspector Willis, at your service. I've come about the, er, situation."

"*Situation*? How astonishing! I had no idea we had a *situation*." I'd finally reached the bottom of the stairs and leaned casually against the balustrade.

Willis wobbled a bit, clearly unsure how to take my comment. Harry, on the other hand, hid a smirk. He was looking rather dashing with fawn colored high pants and a soft red polo shirt. Casual, yet elegant. No wonder Aunt Butty was smitten, though she would never admit such a thing.

"Er, yes. Well...I really must speak with you, Lady Rample," Willis finally managed.

"About?" I arched a brow at him, still playing arrogant aristo to the hilt.

"The *situation*, of course," Harry said helpfully and with a snicker.

"Perhaps you might clarify what this situation is?" I asked as if Aunt Butty and I hadn't already had our noses in police business, with a collection of cobwebs to prove it. Of course, the last person I wanted finding out about our little adventure was the detective in charge. He'd probably lock us up for being busybodies.

"If you would join me in the drawing room," Willis said with all due deference to my station and a bit more bowing and scraping. Though I could tell from the slight scowl between his brows that he wasn't happy about it.

"I'll be out on the veranda if you need me," Harry said. "I think I'll get out the croquet set and get everyone together for a game. Cheerio!" And he exited stage right, as they say—or was it left? In any case, he departed as if his pants were in the proverbial fire and left me to the tender mercies of Brown Suit.

Without another word, I followed Willis into the drawing room, empty at this hour. No doubt the rest of the company were either out and about or recovering from their own grilling. I took a seat on the divan while Willis took a chair opposite me. I noticed that the uniform was sitting on a straight back chair in a shadowy corner, pencil and notebook in hand, looking a little ill at ease. How unobtrusive of him.

"Perhaps you have heard, my lady, that Mr. deVane's study was broken into last night," Willis began after a bit of throat clearing and foot shuffling.

"I hadn't heard, actually," I lied blithely. It may be a failing of mine, but I believe I'm rather accomplished at prevarication. When you grow up as I did, it becomes a matter of self-preservation.

He tapped his pen against his notebook and I noted the dark hair of his eyebrows matched the hair on the back of his knuckles. "Were you not aware the police have been here all morning?" he asked, thick eyebrows rising toward receding hairline.

"As a matter of fact, no."

"And, er, how did you manage to miss that?" His look said he clearly didn't believe me.

"I like to sleep in." I held out my right hand and pretended to study my manicure.

"Until eleven?" he blurted. My blasé attitude was having its desired effect.

"What of it?" Hopefully he wouldn't grill Chaz and discover Aunt Butty and I had been wandering about the garden.

"Right. Well." He harrumphed a bit. "How do you know Mr. deVane?"

"I don't. Not really. My aunt is friends with him—known him for yonks—and he kindly extended an invitation to include me."

Willis nodded as if I'd confirmed what he already knew. "What were your movements last night?"

"From what point?"

He blinked. "Pardon?"

"Do you want to know all about my pre-dinner toilette? The entire conversation at table? Or perhaps my preparations for bed?"

He opened his mouth. Closed it. Finally, he managed, "How about we start with what time you went to bed."

"Very well. It was about one in the morning before I called it quits and went upstairs."

"And was anyone else up at that time?"

"Certainly. Harry...Mr. deVane, was still locked in his study. I assume with Mr. Chamberlain and Lord Varant."

Willis nodded. Clearly, he'd heard that part of the story already. "Go on."

"Chaz, my friend Mr. Raynott, was still in the drawing room along with Miss Semple and Lord Rample."

Confusion marred his brow. "I thought Lord Rample was dead."

"The new Lord Rample. My husband's cousin, Binky."

"Binky?"

"Yes. That's what everyone calls him. Although he's actually called Alphonse Flanders, Lord Rample and whatnot."

He mulled that over. "Right. Anyone else?"

"No. The other guests had all gone to bed already."

"You went up alone?"

I nodded. "I did. Although I did peek in on my aunt to see how she was doing. She was still awake, reading. I bid her goodnight and went to my own room where my maid helped me prepare for bed."

"You brought your own maid?"

"Naturally."

"Er, right. Your maid's name?" Willis asked.

"Maddie."

"Maddie what?"

"Maddie Crewe."

"English?" He seemed surprised. Not that I blamed him. A lot of upper crust matrons preferred maids of the French variety. Not that I considered myself a matron. It sounded so…old and stuffy. But, I suppose, in society's eyes I was, indeed, a matron. Shudder.

"It would seem." The truth was, I knew exactly where Maddie came from, but I wasn't about to tell Willis. She may be a very odd sort for a maid, but she was terribly efficient when necessary. She had a tendency to speak her mind and forget her titles. But only when it suited her. And her secrets, such as they were, weren't mine to tell. Certainly not to a police detective.

"I'll need to speak with her, as well."

"I'm certain that can be arranged," I said blandly. I'd have to advise Maddie not to let on that I'd been out of bed well before the police arrived.

"Did you go to sleep immediately?"

"Very shortly thereafter, yes."

"And did you get up at any point of the night? Hear any odd noises? That sort of thing."

"I'm afraid not, Inspector—"

"Detective Inspector."

"Fair enough. Detective Inspector." It amused me that while he didn't mind flubbing my title, he was very set on me using his properly. Although I suppose in his case he'd rightfully earned it whereas I'd simply married into it. "I slept deeply and well and didn't wake until morning."

He eyed me with suspicion. "Convenient."

"Not really. If I'd known I needed an alibi, I'd have arranged for one." I knew it was poking the bear, so to speak, but I couldn't resist. He practically asked for it.

"You get all that down, Smith?" Willis barked, trying to hide he flush of anger in his cheeks. I'd certainly hit a nerve with this one.

"Yes, sir," the constable in the corner piped.

"Well, then, Lady Rample. I guess you can go."

"Before I do, do you mind telling me what this is all about? Was something stolen?" I asked. I didn't have a lot of hope that DI Willis would blurt out everything he knew but hope springs eternal.

"I'm afraid this is a police matter, Lady Rample," he said gruffly.

"Ah, well, curiosity and all that," I said airily as I rose from the divan and strode toward the door. I spun at the last minute, as though I'd just thought of something. Widening my eyes, I said, "We aren't in danger, are we?"

"Oh, I shouldn't think so, my lady," Willis assured me with that sort of smug superiority such men as he often has toward what they consider the "weaker sex." "Whoever it was shouldn't be back."

"How do you know? How can you be sure?" I asked, batting my eyelashes.

"They got what they came for, didn't they?" the young, uniformed policeman blurted.

Willis shot him a dirty look, and the young constable blushed furiously, ducking his head. Poor man. No doubt he'd get one doozy of a reaming from his superior once I left.

As for me, it did answer one question: Something had been stolen from Harry deVane's office. The question was, what?

"That Willis person is a fiend," Aunt Butty declared as she took a seat across from me. She pulled out a hand fan from somewhere on her person and waved it vigorously.

I was sitting at a small table in a particularly shady spot on the lawn. A light breeze occasionally kicked up, teasing my hair, and making the heat marginally bearable. Chaz, Miss Semple, and the Misses Kettington were playing lawn croquet. Every now and then the smack of wooden mallet against one of the balls echoed across the garden, along with the excited murmur of voices.

Jarvis had informed us that luncheon would be served outside as per Mr. deVane's orders. He hadn't seemed pleased about it, but I thought dining al fresco was a marvelous idea. It was far too hot to be cooped up inside.

I tugged at the scarf around my throat. It was definitely too hot. I loosened the knot, removed the offending fabric, and dropped it over the arm of my chair. "I take it Willis interrogated you, too?"

Her rate of fanning increased with her aggravation. "And how. I gave him a piece of my mind, let me tell you."

I could well imagine. "You didn't mention our little adventure this morning, did you, Aunt?"

"Of course not. Don't be ridiculous," she said, adjusting her floppy straw hat which was decorated with several different colored rosettes and ribbons which dripped down her back. She'd exchanged the trouser outfit for a light cotton dress in rose pink over which she'd tossed a nearly sheer kimono-type garment with wide, flowing sleeves. A pair of round, tortoiseshell sunglasses perched on her small, straight nose. She looked just this side of ridiculous.

A footman marched down the lawn carrying another table. Behind him trailed a couple maids with chairs, Mrs. Bates, her arm laden with linens, and a second footman with a basket, no doubt containing table settings.

Stoically, the footman set up the table and chairs and marched away while the maids quickly draped the table and set it with silver and china. The footman reappeared with another table, and the process repeated itself.

"He wanted to know about Maddie," Aunt Butty said in a low voice.

Something like a cold chill skittered its way down my spine. "Why? She's nothing to do with this."

"Apparently, she's the only one they haven't questioned yet. And she's nowhere to be found. Have you seen her?"

"Not since this morning," I admitted. She'd been gone when we'd returned from the garden, but I hadn't given any thought to it. I hadn't needed her assistance, after all, and took no issue with her filling her time in other ways, as long as she was available when needed. "Perhaps she has...made herself scarce. Not everyone is comfortable talking with the police." And Maddie definitely wouldn't be. Especially not after I'd told her about the spy.

"True," Aunt Butty agreed. "Though she has your protection, and avoiding Willis only makes him the more suspicious. As if that poor girl would have anything to do with whatever nonsense is going on."

I was in full agreement, but well aware the police wouldn't be. "This must have to do with the whole spy situation. I can't see any way around it. Too many coincidences."

"Agreed." Aunt Butty gave a nod that nearly upset her hat. "Though I still find it strange there's a spy in Devon. London I could understand, but we're practically in the middle of nowhere."

At that moment, Harry deVane appeared on the top step, a pipe clenched between his teeth, observing his domain. He'd one hand tucked in his jacket pocket and clutched the pipe with the other. "Butty, my darling!" he crowed, pulling it out of his mouth and waving it about. "What a glorious day." He descended the flagstone steps at a leisurely pace.

"If you can call being grilled by the police glorious," Aunt Butty said drily.

"Really, old girl," he said, pronouncing it "gel" in a sort of upper crust affectation, "it's nothing to get alarmed about." He leaned down to kiss her cheek before taking a seat at our table.

"You don't consider a robbery alarming?" I asked.

He shrugged. "These things happen. What can one do?"

These things did not happen. Well, it wasn't that they *never* happened, but that this particular example was...unusual.

I opened my mouth to ask what had been stolen but was interrupted.

"Is it luncheon yet? I'm half starved," Chaz declared as he appeared from around a hedge. He strolled across the lawn and took the final seat at our table. "I do hope Mrs. Bates has managed something appetizing."

"I'm sure Cook has a glorious repast," Harry assured him. "I told Mrs. Bates to give her free rein."

The other guests drifted over—abandoning the croquet—taking places at the other tables. I caught snippets of conversation, but no one seemed unduly upset by the morning's kerfuffle. Miss Semple was whining about the police wasting her time, but otherwise, no one seemed upset.

Jarvis appeared along with the footmen and a couple maids laden with trays. We were promptly served cold pork pies and beef sandwiches on lovely fresh baked bread with tangy horseradish cream and fresh tomatoes—no doubt from Harry's kitchen garden. This was followed by another lovely summer pudding made with fresh berries and sweet cream. Divine. I ate more than my fair share, I'm not ashamed to admit. The cold lunch was a perfect accompaniment to a hot day.

The conversation was a bit of a disappointment, however. No matter how hard I tried, I couldn't manage to overhear any interesting conversations. And try as she might, Aunt Butty couldn't get Harry to confess the truth about what was really going on or what had been stolen from his study. Instead, he steered the conversation to reminiscences of their past. Which, under normal circumstances might have been interesting, but as things were, I simply couldn't concentrate on anything other than the mystery before me.

Worst of all, in the back of my mind, I'd started to truly worry about Maddie. It wasn't that I believed she had anything to do with the break-in. The idea was preposterous. But her disappearance was too coincidental, and I'd no doubt Willis would look askance upon it. And her.

I needed to find Maddie tout suite. Before she ended up at the wrong end of a police investigation.

Chapter 6

I excused myself immediately after luncheon, beckoning Aunt Butty to follow me. We met in the upper hall outside our rooms.

"Why the cloak and dagger business?" she hissed.

I quickly explained my increasing worries about Maddie. "I need to find her. Get her to talk to Willis before he gets any more suspicious."

"Perhaps you can forestall him. She's been with you for yonks."

"She's only been with me two years. That's hardly yonks." I glanced around. "And if he finds out the truth..."

Aunt Butty's eyes narrowed. "What truth?"

I sighed. I felt I had to tell her. "Maddie was born in Germany."

Now Aunt Butty's eyes widened. "You never told me that. She doesn't have an accent. Well, not a German one."

"Her parents brought her to England when she was a small child. Just before the Great War. She told me the truth when I hired her, of course, but at the time, I found it neither here nor there. Still don't. But Willis might."

"I understand now why he would. If the thief was a German spy—"

"Maddie is not a spy."

"But how do you know?" Aunt Butty insisted. "She could still have ties there."

"Because she's Jewish." There. I'd said it.

Aunt Butty blinked. "Oh. Well, that certainly resolves the spy issue." She seemed completely unfazed about Maddie's origins. Which I should have expected. The rest of the world might turn up their noses, but Aunt Butty never judged a person on her ancestors. After all, according to her, our own ancestors hadn't exactly been entirely upright.

"Right, so we need to find her."

"Yes," Aunt Butty agreed, "although for her sake, she may want to avoid mentioning the German angle."

"No doubt," I said drily. "I'll check the maids' rooms first. Then brave the kitchens."

"Very daring of you. And while you do that, I shall try and get the goods from Harry."

My aunt had been reading American detective stories again. Get the goods, indeed. No doubt she'd get him drunk. Aunt Butty could drink any man under the table. She claimed she'd learned a few tricks whilst visiting a friend in Dublin. I had no doubt of it.

The servants' quarters were in the attic, four flights up. By the time I reached the top of the somewhat rickety staircase, I had a stitch in my side and was feeling a bit winded. I could dance all night if the mood struck, but stairs were the Devil's work.

At the top of the stairs was a long, narrow hall with doors on either side. I'd no idea which room was

Maddie's, so I knocked on the first door. When I got no answer, I pushed it open. The room was painted stark white, with no adornments save a wooden cross on the wall, just a bare wood floor and a narrow cot for a bed. Next to the bed was a stand holding a cheap lamp and a ragged copy of the Bible. A wash stand stood in one corner and there were pegs for hanging clothes, one empty and one containing what looked like a dress for Sunday best and a simple straw hat. Depressing.

The next room was much the same, save instead of a cross there were magazine cutouts of a couple of well-known actors and actresses, and instead of a Bible there was a romance novel with a rather lurid cover. I approved.

And so on down the hall. The smallest, ugliest room of all was clearly Maddie's. She appeared to be sharing it with one of the maids. I recognized the book on the floor next to a camp cot as one from my own library, and the Sunday best dress and hat on the spare hook as Maddie's own. But of Maddie there was no sign.

I tromped down the many flights of stairs to the kitchen. The clanging of pots assailed my ears and the yeasty scent of fresh-baked bread teased my nose as I rounded a corner. I popped my head through the doorway. At first no one noticed.

The woman I assumed was "Cook" was bent over the stove, tasting something bubbling in a pot. Her wide backside stretched her gray uniform dress to the utmost and the large apron wrapped around her middle was well worn and more off-white than white. Next to her, a nervous young girl in a matching oversized apron fidgeted. There was no one else in the room.

"Does it taste alright?" the girl asked in a high-pitched, nervous tone. Her large eyes protruded slightly from a narrow face and her overbite could have given Binky a run for his money.

The cook smacked her lips. "Needs salt." She pinched some from a bowl next to the stove, added it, and gave the pot a stir. Another sample and, "That'll do it."

They both turned at that moment and spotted me. Cook frowned mightily, the heavy features of her face making her look positively fearsome. "Your ladyship shouldn't be down here. Not proper."

"I'm looking for my maid. Maddie. Have you seen her?" I asked, ignoring proprieties as I often did.

"No, m'lady. Have you, Joany?" Cook fixed a glare on the young girl.

Joany looked like she might faint. "N-no, Cook. Not since this morning."

I sighed. "Oh, dear. I really must speak to her. I don't suppose the other maids have seen her?"

"They're about their duties, m'lady. No time to be babysitting some, ah, anyone," Cook said firmly.

"Right. Well, thanks ever so." I gave them an airy wave and headed back upstairs, unsure where to search next. The library, perhaps? Maddie always did like hiding out in mine, such as it was. I imagined that a proper library in a manor such as this must be irresistible.

The library was next door to Harry's study. The study door was closed, and I wondered if the police were done...doing whatever it was they did. I hadn't seen or heard them leave, but that meant nothing in this massive house.

I pushed open the door of the library, straining to see in the dim light streaming from the tiny gap in the curtains. Either the maids were shirking their duties, or Harry was very devoted to protecting his books.

And there, huddled in the window seat, was Maddie. Nose in a book. She glanced up, eyes wide, when I let the door shut behind me.

"Lady Rample!" She scrambled from the seat, dumping a book on the floor in her haste to curtsey.

"Maddie. I've been looking everywhere for you."

"Sorry, my lady. I figured you and your aunt were off and I wasn't needed." She glanced around guiltily.

"Normally that would be the case, but...didn't you hear about the break-in last night?"

She shrugged. "Sure. But what's it got to do with me?"

I sighed. "The police want to question everyone that was here. Including you."

"But I don't know anything!" Maddie wailed.

"True. But if you don't speak with them, they might grow suspicious." If they weren't already.

"Will you come with me, Miss? I mean, Lady Rample?"

"I suppose. If I must." It likely wouldn't hurt, and I could insure Willis didn't get out of hand. "I'm not certain they're still here. The police I mean."

"Then I could just stay here," Maddie said brightly.

"Don't be daft. We need to make sure the police know you're willing to cooperate. Now come along." I strode out without looking back, expecting her to follow me. She hesitated, then I finally heard her footsteps behind me. I paused a moment and turned to her. "One thing, Maddie. You brought me my tea at half past ten in the morning and didn't leave my room until gone eleven. Right?"

"But that's a lie, m'lady," she said, giving me a shrewd look.

"Yes. Yes, it is."

Not knowing where else to go, I rapped on Harry's study door. There was a shuffling sound from the other side, then the door swung open to reveal the suspicious visage of DI Willis.

"Detective Inspector," I said, "you wished to speak to my maid?"

"What of it?" he snarled.

I restrained myself from throttling him. "I've brought her. Maddie."

Maddie stepped forward looking nervous and a little ill. I think if the floor had opened her up and swallowed her in that moment, she would have been thrilled. As it was, she just fidgeted.

Willis narrowed gimlet eyes as he scanned Maddie up and down. He clearly found her lacking. "Very good. This way." He slipped out of the study, shutting the door so quickly I hardly got a glimpse inside.

Shoving past me, he led us back toward the drawing room, currently unoccupied. This late in the afternoon the guests were either napping, enjoying a shady spot somewhere, or perhaps down at the boat house enjoying a swim. And my guess was that a couple of the male guests had gone to the pub in the village to while away the afternoon over an ale or several.

Willis tried to shoo me out, but I was having none of it. "She's my maid. I will stay and hear what she has to say."

"Fine," he snarled. He muttered something about "toffs" which I chose to ignore. Really, I'd half a mind to report him to his superiors. His attitude was simply uncalled for.

He beckoned Maddie to sit, but she shook her head. "I prefer to stand, sir."

He harrumphed. "Very well. Why weren't you available for questioning this morning?"

"Sorry, sir, I was unaware I was wanted." Maddie's expression was completely blank to the point of being stupid. Which she bloody well wasn't. I gave an inner cheer for her cleverness. Willis expected her to be stupid, so stupid she was.

"Listen, girl, you should always make yourself available to the police."

"Yes, sir. Sorry, sir." She blinked slowly, giving him cow eyes, ramping up the idiot role.

I held back a snicker. "I think she's learned her lesson, Detective Inspector. Let's get on with it, shall we?"

He glared at me but did as requested. "What were your movements last night, girl?"

"My movements, sir?" Maddie repeated stupidly.

"Yes, girl, your movements. What did you do last night after Lady Rample came upstairs from tea?"

He meant supper, of course. Tea being a term more commonly used among the so-called "lower classes." My own father referred to the evening meal as "tea," lowly vicar that he is.

"Well..." Maddie drug the word out as if she were just discovering it. "Lady Rample come up late, you see, from wot she usually does."

"How late?" he asked, eyeing me sharply.

"'Bout one in the morning, sir. I'd fallen asleep, you see. And she scolded me."

"Right. Fell asleep where?'

"In her room, sir. On the sofa thingy."

"The chaise longue," I supplied.

"What the blue blazes is a chase long?" he snapped.

"It's a—"

"Never mind." He shook his head and turned back to Maddie. "So, you fell asleep, Lady Rample woke you up, then what?"

"I helped her get ready for bed, then I went up to bed myself. I was that tired."

"What time was that?" He jotted something in his notebook.

"I dunno, sir. Around two, mayhap."

She was laying the dumb routine on thick. "Yes, about that."

"Right. Then what?"

Maddie blinked again, slowly. "Why, I don't know, sir. I went to sleep."

"And after you slept?" he gritted out.

"Woke up at eight, as per my usual when away from home. Went for a walk, got my breakfast, then went about work. Woke Lady Rample at half ten with her morning tea. Was with her 'til gone eleven," she parroted my words almost exactly.

He sighed and rubbed his forehead. "You didn't get up during the night at any time?"

"No, sir."

"Didn't hear anything or see anything unusual?"

"No, sir."

He sighed again. "And can anyone vouch for your whereabouts during the night?"

"I s'pose Mary can."

"That's Mary, one of the household maids?"

"Yes, sir. I share a room with her."

"Right then. That will be all." He didn't bother to thank either of us but shooed us out with a motion of his hand.

"What an unutterable ass," I muttered as I shut the door firmly behind us.

"Goodness, m'lady, language! What would your aunt say?"

"The same, no doubt."

"Is it over, m'lady?"

I nodded. "Yes, Maddie." At least I jolly well hoped so. If only we were closer to knowing the truth.

Chapter 7

I spent the rest of the day in my room trying alternatively to nap or read. Neither worked. My mind buzzed and fizzed with possibilities. Finally, I gave up and dressed early for supper. Since Maddie wasn't there to help, I donned a simple light green satin evening dress. The bodice was loose enough to fit my ample bosoms, and the straps were decorated with sparkling rhinestones. Slipping my feet into silver sandals, I waited with one ear to the door as the other guests tucked themselves away in their rooms to prepare for the evening. Then I slipped downstairs.

Detective Inspector Willis had left hours ago, ostensibly to return to the station and report to his superiors. Unfortunately, Harry had been locked in his study the rest of the day, so it had been off limits. This was my first chance to snoop...Er, investigate.

The lock on the study door proved as difficult to pick as the one on the cellar door had. I was about to give up in frustration when someone loomed over me and said, "Want me to have a go?"

I glanced up. "Chaz! Give a girl heart palpitations, why don't you. Why aren't you getting ready?" At some point he'd swapped out his seersucker suit for a white dinner jacket over black trousers.

"Didn't need much doing, darling. Quick change and voila." He spread his hands as if to indicate his magnificence. "And I saw you slipping out. Knew you'd be up to no good. Spy hunting, are we?"

"Trying to. Could you?" I held up the pick set.

He waved me aside and had the lock open in minutes.

We both slipped inside and shut the door behind us. Straight ahead were a pair of French windows, no doubt the same ones the burglar had broken into, overlooking the main gardens and the path wending down the hillside to the river and the boathouse. To the left was a large window which overlooked the side gardens and the orangery. The curtains were back on both, though sheer drapes covered them with a light filmy gauze, leaving the room in soft twilight. The scent of pipe smoke lingered, and underneath, the faintest trace of men's cologne. Something expensive and citrusy. Not unlike what Chaz wore.

To the right was a modern fireplace, neatly appointed with a carved mantlepiece and art deco tiles. In front of that was a single reading chair, simple lines covered in wine velvet, and a side table perfect for setting one's drink on while reading the paper or a book.

In the middle of the room stood a large antique desk which could have stood in for a dining table. The thing was vast. On it were several stacks of papers and folders of varying heights. Behind it was a leather chair. Against the wall to the left of the French doors was a filing cabinet and a small bookshelf containing not books, but file boxes, all neatly labeled.

"Doesn't look like there's been a break-in," Chaz mused.

"I imagine the maids have been in to clean," I said. "Harry no doubt had them in the minute Willis was out the door."

"So we've no idea what the place looked like after the supposed burglary."

I glanced at him, surprised by his words. "What do you mean? Do you think Harry faked the break-in?"

He shrugged. "Anything's possible. Don't you think it's odd that Neville Chamberlain, of all people, was here, and then next thing there's a burglary, but Harry has no idea if anything was taken?"

"He does? But the constable—Smith, I think—slipped up and said something had been taken."

Chaz shrugged. "If that's true, then dear Harry is lying through his very white teeth."

It was dashed odd. "Do you think it was a cover up? But why? What would Harry be trying to cover up?"

"Damned if I know. Maybe he isn't. Maybe the constable was confused. Or trying to sound important. But it's just...odd."

Odd it was. "Well, let's just look around and see if we can learn anything of use."

"Where should we start?"

I tapped my chin. "I'll have a look at the papers on the desk. You check out the file cabinet and the bookshelf. We only have perhaps twenty minutes before the first guests come down for pre-supper drinks."

"Less. Harry usually gets down first."

"Dash it all. Fifteen, then."

We went to work, quickly thumbing through papers, trying to get some idea of what Harry was up to. Most of the papers on the desk were farm documents: ledgers, notes from tenants, orders of seed. That sort of thing. There were also bank statements, correspondence between Harry and various people—some personal, some clearly business. But nothing that gave any indication as to why someone would want to break into his study.

Chaz was still deep in the file cabinet, so I roamed the edge of the room. Maybe something had fallen under a chair or behind a bookshelf? But I found nothing. Until I came to the fireplace.

It had been decidedly hot over the past few days. Far too hot to have a fire going. But there, in the grate, were the charred remains of just such a thing.

I knelt down, frowning. Even if Harry had been cold and decided to start a fire, surely the maids would have been in to clean by now?

Using the poker, I carefully nudged some of the ash to the side, catching sight of something not entirely burned. It was a small bit of paper with something neatly drawn. Schematics of some sort, it looked like, but it was hard to say; the piece was so small.

Before I could show it to Chaz, I heard a familiar voice in the hallway. I froze, hoping Harry would simply head into the drawing room. Instead, footsteps echoed outside the door. Without thinking, I dashed across the room, grabbed Chaz by the arm, and yanked him toward the French doors.

We barely made it outside and out of eyeline of anyone entering the room, before the study door swung open and Harry could be heard saying, "...I've got one in here. Let me show you..."

I carefully reached over and pushed the French door closed until it latched softly. Then I took a deep breath and stepped away, down the side of the house with Chaz hot on my heels.

"That was close," he said.

"Too close," I agreed. "Did you find anything?"

"Not a thing," he said cheerfully. "Just bally boring ledgers and such. No secret government documents. What about you?"

I told him about the fragment I'd found in the fireplace. "I have no idea what it was, and it might not mean anything," I admitted. "I just think it's suspicious that he burned it in the fireplace in the middle of the summer instead of throwing it away in the bin."

"Does seem deuced odd." Chaz shoved his hands in his pockets. "What now?"

I sighed. "I don't know. I need to have a think. Why don't you go on in?"

"What about you?"

"I'm going to take a turn around the garden. Maybe head down to the river. A bit of solitude would do me good." The sun had sunk low on the horizon and it was finally a tolerable temperature. Fresh air was just the thing to clean out the cobwebs.

"While you're gone, I'll see if I can't rustle up a proper highball for you."

"Actually, I think I'm off highballs for the moment. How about another one of those marvelous Aviation cocktails?"

He winked and strode toward the terrace and the doors leading into the drawing room.

I slipped further into the garden, losing myself down a winding path edged in masses of roses, rhododendrons, lavender, larkspur, and lilies. Wisteria and climbing roses had even been trained over arched trellises so they formed a tunnel of color and perfume. Bees buzzed to and fro and the occasional humming bird zipped in to sip from one of the blooms. I almost wished I lived in the country, so I could have such a garden, but I was a city girl through and through. The occasional visit to the countryside was fine but give me the bright lights of London any day. I needed people and excitement and things to do, places to go.

The path curved downward toward the river and I followed it. The air got cooler and damper as I descended. Perhaps I should have brought a shawl with me.

The path came to an end at a small promontory edged in a low rock wall before descending again toward the boat house. I could just see its roof through the trees.

I stepped closer to the wall. The view over the River Dart was splendid. Distant lights shone like fireflies as the sun sank into the sea to my right, coloring the sky in rose and orange.

I tried to bring my mind back to the matter at hand, but it would wander down the garden path, so to speak. Perhaps I should give this silliness up. No one had been hurt. Harry even claimed nothing had been taken, despite what Constable Smith had claimed. And Willis seemed to believe Maddie's story, so I no longer feared she was in danger. The policeman no doubt believed her to be just another English lass gone into service and had no idea of her background. I'd worried for nothing. So, yes, maybe I should just give up my little investigation and let the police handle things. The likelihood was my curiosity would never be satiated anyway. I might as well enjoy this time. Perhaps a trip to the sea was in order? It was just a short bit away.

"Penny for your thoughts?"

I froze. I knew that voice. But it couldn't be. He was away in France, playing jazz in Paris, no doubt. And yet...

I turned slowing, drinking in the sight of him. Broad shoulders. Bedroom eyes. Full lips that knew just how to kiss. I'd had personal experience with that.

I stepped closer and he reached out to stroke a hand down my arm, his long, artist's fingers so dark against my pale, bare skin. I managed to hold back a sigh, but only just.

"Hale," I finally managed. "You're here. How—?"

"We can talk about the how later. Right now, I've more important things to do." And he pulled me tight against him and kissed me. At first it was soft and sweet, full of lush promise. But then it grew a bit steamier and more intense.

Just when I thought I might do something embarrassing like swoon, he let me go and skimmed a finger down my cheek. "Been dreaming of that for a while."

His husky voice twinned with that American accent almost had me swooning all over again. I reminded myself sternly that I was a grown woman and didn't go swooning over musicians. Or anyone, for that matter.

"What are you doing here?" I finally managed.

The last I'd seen of Hale Davis had been at the Astoria Club, one of London's premier jazz clubs. Since it was now shut down, thanks to a murder on site, he and his jazz band had moved to greener pastures. Not that I blamed him. Musicians had to go where there were people willing to hire them, and in his case, the people willing to hire him were in France.

I admit I'd wished he'd stayed, that we could have spent more time together, but the reality was that despite mutual attraction, we came from two different worlds. Didn't mean I missed him any less, or that I was any less annoyed that he didn't write. Or call. Or something.

He grinned and rocked back on his heels, tucking his hands into the pockets of his high-waisted white trousers. He was dressed all in white which stood out against his dark skin and made him seem equal parts dapper and dangerous. "Man said there was a party and he wanted music. So, here I am."

"Mr. deVane hired you? When did you get back from France?" And why hadn't he contacted me?

"Couple days. Don't worry, I was going to look you up." He had the audacity to smolder at me.

"Who said I was worried?" I said archly.

He gave me a knowing look that was somewhat cheeky, although he did have me pegged. He knew exactly how he affected me. I wasn't used to someone else having the upper hand. I wasn't sure I cared for it.

One could say my former husband Felix had been the one with the upper hand. Older, wealthier, and worldlier, while I was hardly more than a girl from an impoverished, albeit somewhat aristocratic, background. Well, if I were honest, I wasn't exactly "hardly more than a girl." I'd been in my late twenties. On the shelf, as it were. But the truth of the matter was that Felix and I had been equals. He'd been quite the feminist. Surprising for a man of his age and station.

"Are you here for long?" I asked Hale, hoping he would say that he was.

He wrapped an arm around me and guided me to a bench built into the wall and half hidden beneath a weeping willow. "Through the weekend. My new band is joining me for the big shindig at the end."

The costume party and dance Harry had promised. I had been rather blasé about it before, but now it held a new level of excitement. I reminded myself that this was never going to go anywhere and that Varant was a more suitable suitor, but apparently, I wasn't listening to myself. For all his sex appeal, Varant never gave me goose pimples.

"Good," I said awkwardly. "Why didn't you write?" I instantly cursed myself for being a simpering idiot. I hadn't meant to sound so…needy.

Hale shrugged. "We had a great time, but it was...brief. I didn't think I'd ever be back here. Seemed right that I should let you move on. Find someone...more like that Lord you were spending time with."

"Varant. He's here, you know." I figured I might as well warn him. Avoid any awkwardness.

"Yes. I heard." Hale's tone was dry, but his face gave no indication one way or the other how he felt about Varant.

"I don't plan on marrying again," I blurted. "I like my freedom. Sorry, I don't know why I told you that. But it's true. I had one husband and that was enough."

"Did you love him that much? That you would stay true to him?"

"Who? Felix?" I laughed softly. "Felix was a dear and I adored him, but it wasn't the grand passion you imagine. We enjoyed each other's company, supported each other's endeavors, and cared for each other, but we weren't madly in love or anything. No, I plan to remain unmarried because I prefer my freedom."

"How does Varant feel about that?"

"No idea. Don't particularly care, either. But I imagine it would make me much less desirable to him." Which might explain his coolness. Perhaps he realized I would never want anything permanent from him. He really should marry a biddable girl who would give him oodles of heirs.

"Not sure he sees it that way," Hale warned.

"Yes, well..." How had we gotten on the subject? "In any case, it's very noble of you to shove me off onto some other man, but I assure you, it was entirely unnecessary. And rather cheeky, if I do say so. What makes you think I needed to 'move on' as you say?"

The look he gave me made my stomach flutter. As he leaned in the flutters moved lower.

"Let me show you."

Oh, my.

Chapter 8

I had just finished breakfast the next morning and was making my way toward the library when Miss Semple accosted me. She wore cream colored trousers with a matching cream halter top which left her impossibly pale shoulders bare. She held a floppy cream and navy hat in one hand and a pair of large, round sunglasses in the other.

"Aren't you coming?" She eyed me from beneath heavily kohled eyelids. Her face was rather too narrow and her nose too long for true beauty, but she had an interesting face.

"Coming where?" I asked.

"To the fete in Stickleberry. It's not really my thing, you know, but it's so deadly dull around here that I am willing to do simply *anything*."

"I see. I hadn't realized there was a fete." And I was surprised that Harry, as a local landowner, didn't have something to do with it. Generally, such a personage as Harry would be roped into opening the thing at the very least. Possibly even judging who had the largest pig or who had baked the best spice cake.

"Down in the village. Church thing, I imagine." She yawned. "So, are you coming? Binky is going to drive us down."

I wondered if she'd given up on Harry and had set her hat for Binky. If so, she was going to have an unpleasant surprise. Other than the manor house up north—which was entailed—poor Binky didn't have a proverbial pot to piss in.

"Actually, it's a beautiful day, so I think I'll walk to Sickleberry."

She shrugged, pursing her crimson lips. "Suit yourself."

I watched as she toddled out the open front door on rather perilous heels. Not exactly suitable footwear for a country church fete.

A shiny red convertible pulled up, and Binky honked the horn. Where did he get a posh car like that? There was no way the estate produced enough money for that sort of thing. It barely sustained itself.

I narrowed my gaze in thought. Could he have something to do with the break-in? Perhaps he'd resorted to a life of crime in order to get his hands on the sort of funds needed for the lifestyle he felt he deserved.

Pushing that thought aside—Binky hadn't the brains for such machinations—I went off to find my aunt.

"Dear girl," she said when I asked if she wanted to accompany me to the fete, "I would rather have my liver eaten by buzzards."

"That seems rather drastic," I said dryly.

She narrowed her eyes. "Why would you want to go? I'd have thought you'd have enough of such affairs to last a lifetime."

She was right. My father was the village vicar in the town of Chipping Poggs. I'd attended many a church fete in my time. One of the few enjoyments I was allowed growing up.

"It seems something to do. Besides, it might give me a chance to ask around about the break-in."

"You're back on that, are you?"

"Nothing else to do."

She gave me a knowing look. "Harry told me he hired a musician for the rest of the week. I believe you know him."

"Yes, I saw him last night."

"I see." Her eyes twinkled.

I must have blushed fiery red. "Do you?"

"Those Americans...such enthusiastic lovers, don't you think?"

"Aunt!" I gasped.

She cackled merrily and shooed me from her rooms. "Have fun. And don't do anything I wouldn't do."

That left an awfully lot of room for shenanigans.

Since I couldn't find Chaz, I decided to walk to the fete on my own. It would give me a chance to process my thoughts. I had planned to give up my investigation of the break-in, but honestly, something was niggling at me. I just wasn't sure what. In the back of my mind I kept seeing that piece of burned paper. What did it mean?

The path to the church wound through the manor house grounds, keeping mostly beneath the trees, making for a pleasant, shady walk. I strolled slowly enjoying the hum of bees, the lowing of cows, the green scent of hot sun on grass, and the light breeze on my skin.

Footsteps sounded behind me on the path, startling me out of my reverie and sending a shiver of apprehension through me. I whirled to find a familiar figure striding toward me.

"Hale." It came out a little more breathless that I intended.

"Ophelia." He swooped down and planted one on me, leaving me even more breathless. "I thought I might join you on your walk. If you don't mind."

"No, of course not."

He offered his arm and I took it. It felt right to be walking beside him like this, heart racing, mind buzzing, body thrumming.

I heard the off-key cacophony of the village brass band floating across the meadow as we neared the church, its spire poking up above the trees like a spindle through green wool. "Oh, dear, someone really should tell them they sound dreadful," I mused.

Hale chuckled. "Let them have their fun."

"That's awfully magnanimous coming from a professional."

"We all had to start somewhere," he said.

I started when he gently dropped my arm and stepped away. I glanced at him, askance, wondering what was wrong.

"You go ahead. We shouldn't be seen together."

I frowned. For a moment I felt the sting of rejection and wondered daftly if it was because of the investigation. Or perhaps Varant. Surely, Hale hadn't gone off me already. Then I realized. In London, such things were—if not completely approved of—regular. After the Great War, there were few single, young, white men left. So English women found love where they could, regardless of race. But this was a small village. There would be those who wouldn't approve of our closeness, and they'd take it out not on me—someone who could defend myself not perhaps with muscles, but with money and friends in high places. No, they'd take it out on Hale, a stranger in a strange land and a black man to boot.

I sighed. "I wish things were different."

He gave me a lopsided grin. "I do, too. Maybe someday they will be."

I nodded, wondering if there were something I *could* do. Perhaps Aunt Butty would have an idea. She knew so many people and had been so many places, she always had excellent ideas.

"Alright then. I'll go on alone. For now." I gave him a saucy wink, and sashayed off, no doubt his gaze was firmly fixed on my rather curvaceous backside. It might not concede to popular fashion, but I'd never had any complaints from the male gender.

The fete was much as I'd imagined. A large sign above the entrance to the churchyard proclaimed the fete was to support a local orphan charity. Tables had been set up manned by the village ladies. Some had goods for sale:

homemade jams and jellies, crocheted doilies, knitted socks, pies, biscuits. Others had games—such as tombola—for prizes no doubt donated by parishioners: a bottle of homemade summer wine, tins of peaches, a fresh baked pound cake. A bric-a-brac stall had various used items for sale such as books and gently worn clothes.

Off to the side was the white tea tent where one could purchase a cuppa and a slice of homemade cake. Across from it was the temporary bandstand where every local villager who owned a musical instrument had gathered to show off their talents—such as they were. I winced at a particularly vile-sounding note.

Next to the tambola stand was a tent draped in colorful cloth. A hand painted sign out front read: Madame Mystic's Palm Reading—2p.

I grinned. Perhaps Madame Mystic would have some useful information to impart.

I ducked inside to find the standard round table covered in cheap, velvet cloth behind which sat a middle-aged woman. Her hair had been done up in a purple turban and she wore what looked like a cape made of old curtains.

"Please, sit," she said in a fake accent, probably meant to mimic the Romany.

I took the chair across from her and laid a couple coins on the table. She inspected them closely and nodded.

"Give me your hand."

I held out my hand, palm up, and she took it in a surprisingly strong grip. Yanking it closer she inspected my hand, grunting a little now and then.

"Well?" I asked lightly. "What do you see?"

She curved a jagged nail along a line in my palm. "Long life, you see."

"Ah, yes. How interesting."

"And this…children. Three. No four."

I held back a snort. Not likely. "Hmmm."

Then she let out a small gasp. "Be careful milady. Very careful."

I lifted a brow. "Do you see danger?"

"Of the heart." She gave me a shrewd look. "Juggling two men can be dangerous business."

I smiled tightly. Wondering how she knew. "I'll take that under advisement. Anything else?"

Her nose was almost to my palm when she suddenly reared back. "Beware the masked woman."

"What's that supposed to mean?"

She shrugged and dropped my hand. "No idea. I just read the palms, I don't interpret them. That's all. You can go."

Amused, I exited the tent and caught sight of Miss Semple and Binky in the tea-tent. I immediately turned the other way and ducked into the bric-a-brac stall. I wouldn't mind having a chat with Miss Semple, but I would prefer to avoid my cousin-in-law.

I was eyeballing a worn paperback of *The Murder of Roger Ackroyd* when I saw movement out of the corner of my eye. I glanced toward the church—a medieval stone monstrosity—and saw a man slip around the corner out of sight. I frowned.

It wasn't so much the man himself who'd caught my attention. It was his furtiveness. He'd glanced around as if trying to escape notice. How odd. And then there was the fact he'd been wearing a bowler hat. Which didn't mean anything, of course. Lot's of men wore bowler hats, but I couldn't help but recall that the man skulking around the garden the night of the break-in had been wearing such a hat.

Overwhelmed by curiosity, I shoved some money at the lady running the booth, crammed the book into my handbag, and slipped out after the man. Rounding the corner of the church, I found no one in sight.

Letting out a sound of frustration, I hurried down the side of the church. To my left was the stone wall, warm from the sun, unbroken at this level as the window sills were nearly above my head. To the right was a row of trees bobbing slightly in a light summer breeze. A butterfly fluttered a little too close to my face.

There was nowhere for the man to have escaped. No doors for him to duck into. And the way into the wood was barred by a split-rail fence. Granted, he could have hopped over it, but then why duck behind the church? I kept going.

Finally, I came to the end of the wall and turned left. The back door of the church stood open slightly, letting in fresh air and sunlight. I stepped through the doorway, squinting to let my eyes adjust. I found myself standing in a small room that looked like it doubled as a dressing room and storage space. A second door, also open, lead to the sanctuary.

I strode quickly to the open door and peered through. Inside the small sanctuary were about half a dozen or so rows of pews. Sitting to one side, halfway toward the front, was the man I'd seen sneaking around the church. And next to him was a second man, his back to me. They huddled together whispering quietly, expressions intense. I couldn't make out what they were saying; they spoke too low and the echoing room distorted their voices.

Finally, they finished their discussion and stood to leave. I almost gasped aloud. The second man was Binky! Why would Binky have a secret assignation with a strange man at a church in a village where he'd never been before? Dashed odd, if you ask me.

But something about it seemed very...off. I felt a sudden chill go through me and decided it would be the better part of valor to remove myself from the area immediately.

I had just returned to the fete when dark clouds began together overhead. There was an ominous rumble of thunder. I ducked into the tea tent just as the sky opened up and rain poured down.

Miss Semple sat alone, sipping a cup of tea and picking at a piece of cake. I sat down next to her. "Lovely weather we're having."

"Typical English summer. I should have gone to the Riviera."

"Oh, yes? You have a house there?" I doubted it, based on what I'd heard of her family's finances.

"I have many friends who would love for me to stay with them," she said a tad tartly. I felt a bit badly for offending her.

"How lovely for you," I murmured politely, deciding not to mention my own little villa. No doubt Binky had already moaned about it. Possibly why she was a bit sore.

The tea lady arrived with a cup of tea and a slice of cake on neat, if cheap, china. I thanked her and took a sip. The tea was well done, indeed, and the ginger cake a marvel. Moist and sticky, and ever so sweet with just the right amount of vanilla icing. I decided to ask the lady if I could get another slice or two before I left.

"Where's Binky got to?" I asked Miss Semple, as if I didn't already know.

"Heaven knows," she said. "I think he wanted to try his hand at the tambola. Whatever for, I wonder? It's not like a Lord needs tinned peaches."

I wondered as well, because I was certain Binky had been nowhere near the tambola. I was becoming increasingly suspicious of my dear cousin-in-law all the time.

"How do you know Harry deVane?" I asked, deciding to learn more about Miss Semple while I had the chance.

That got her going. She launched into a long and overly-dramatic story about how her "dear papa" had met "dear, dear Harry" and how he—Harry—had fallen madly in love with her. I somehow figured it was the other way around, but I wasn't about to point that out. I didn't think Miss Semple would take it terribly well. She seemed a bit…mercurial.

"So you're not interested in Binky?" I asked.

She shrugged one shoulder. "He'd make a good backup. Just in case I can't get Harry to cooperate."

Damnation. Well, this was as good a time as any to warn her. "You know he's dead broke, right?"

For a split second she looked crestfallen. "Dash it. Well, at least I'd be a lady. That's something."

"Sure," I agreed heartily. "Stuck in a crumbling manor house in the far north of England."

"No townhouse?" She leaned forward, aghast.

"Afraid not."

She slumped back in her seat. "Well isn't that just my luck."

Poor Miss Semple. She certainly didn't seem to be having much luck with her choices in suitors.

At last the rain stopped, the sky cleared, and the sun returned, turning the soupy ground into steamy, muddy muck. The air grew hot and humid and I felt myself wilting slightly.

I was about to beg my leave when Binky joined us. Was it just me, or was he looking rather shifty and nervous? Beads of sweat lined his upper lip and his forehead under the brim of his fedora. Could be the heat. Or could be something else entirely.

He gave me the side-eye. "Ophelia. What are you doing here?"

"Thought I'd check out the fete. But it's all gone to rubbish, darling. Don't you think?" I played the languid and dimwitted ingénue rather well, I thought. Perhaps I should seek a career on the silver screen.

"We should probably go back to the house," Miss Semple agreed. "It's too, too hot. And the mud is ghastly. I fear I shall ruin my Ferragamos."

"I suppose you need a ride," Binky said to me. Rather ungraciously, I thought.

"Too kind, darling. Don't mind if I do." Perhaps I could get something out of him on the ride home.

Alas, it wasn't to be. Binky drove like a maniac through the country roads, nearly crashing into a tractor in the process. We fishtailed around corners and bumped over potholes with great enthusiasm. It was all I could do to keep my seat and hold onto my hat. If Aunt Butty ever had the pleasure of riding with Binky, she'd never complain about my driving again.

He pulled up to the front door in a screeching halt and exited the vehicle, storming into the house without bothering to assist either myself or Miss Semple.

"Well, I never!" The other woman managed to extricate herself from the car, although she nearly toppled into a mud puddle in the process. "I need a drink."

"I'm with you. I think an Aviation is in order, don't you?" Interrogating Binky would have to wait.

Chapter 9

Miss Semple draped herself across the divan cushions and waited expectantly while I mixed two Aviation cocktails, carefully measuring out the costly crème de violette. I handed her one, then took the comfy chair across from her.

"Miss Semple—"

"Call me Julia."

"Julia then. And I'm Ophelia."

"What a lovely name," she said, taking a sip of her cocktail. "Very Shakespearean."

"Isn't it just. Are you friends with my cousin-in-law?"

She blinked, ridiculously long lashes brushing perfectly powdered porcelain cheek. Her lashes had to be false. Had to be. "Cousin-in-law?"

"Binky."

"Oh! Lord Rample. He's your cousin?"

"In-law. The cousin of my late husband."

"I thought perhaps you were Lord Rample's mother," she said innocently.

I have never in my life wanted to strangle someone so much. Julia and I were of an age—mid-30s, give or take—and if anything, I looked younger. Extra padding will do that. But I bit my tongue. Bees with honey. And Julia Semple certainly had a stinger.

"Not quite," I managed to bite out. "He's actually older than I by a good four years."

She widened her eyes. "How astonishing."

I wondered if Aunt Butty had brought any laxative with her and if she would let me borrow some to put in this Semple woman's tea. "I'm sure. So... how long have you known Binky?"

"I only met him here for the first time." She took a sip of her cocktail and made an approving hum. My estimation of her went up slightly. "I believe Harry knows him."

Harry deVane didn't know Binky. He knew Aunt Butty. And somehow Binky had wormed his way to an invite based on his vague relation to her. The thought irked me.

"Frankly, I don't know why he came," Julia continued. "Claims the whole thing is an awful bore. He's not wrong. Dashedly dull. But one doesn't *say* that, does one."

So why did he worm an invite then? Curious. "If it's so dull, why did you come?" I asked.

"Harry, of course. He's worth simply millions. And, of course, I have the most awfully mad crush on him," she added quickly.

Crush on his aforementioned millions, more like. We chatted inanely about various people we knew and events we had attended, but the minute my glass was drained, I made my excuses and escaped. Now to find Binky.

He was hiding in the library. Not because he was a great reader. He was listening to the radio and pounding down a bottle of whiskey he'd liberated from Harry's cellar.

"There you are," I said, shutting the door behind me.

He frowned. "What do you want?" His tone was querulous and his words slightly slurred. If the bottle was anything to go by, he was well on his way to raging drunk.

"Why are you here, Binky?"

"I'm drinking, obviously." He waved a glass at me, nearly sloshing the contents onto his jacket.

"No, I mean *here*, at this house. At this party."

"Oh, that...Harry begged me to come."

"Don't lie, Binky. It doesn't become you. I know you used Aunt Butty's name to finagle yourself an invite. Why?"

"If you must know, I had business to attend to in this part of the country. And, thanks to your late husband, I don't have the funds for a hotel. What else was I to do?" He downed the liquor and poured himself another.

I sat in the chair next to him. "I see. So this is simply a matter of saving money. Free lodging. Free food. Free booze."

"Of course. What else?"

"How about that man I saw you talking to at the church?"

I think he paled slightly, but it was hard to tell beneath the flush of alcohol. "I have no idea what you're talking about." His hand shook slightly as he poured himself another drink.

"You're a terrible liar, Binky. Felix always said so."

"Leave my cousin out of this," he snarled. "He's the reason I'm in this mess."

"What mess?"

Unfortunately, while Binky wasn't the brightest, he was smart enough to clam up. "Leave me in peace, Ophelia. I've nothing more to say to you."

And that, as they say, was that. At least for now. But I was determined to get the truth out of him. One way or another.

Dinner that night was a somewhat somber affair. It was only the house guests, and everyone seemed either focused on the discomfort of the heat and humidity, or the break-in, which appeared to instill equal parts fear and excitement.

"Things like this never happen where we come from," Maude Breverman whispered over dinner. She was seated to my left and wanted to talk about nothing more than the break-in. She likely didn't have much excitement in her life. "It's rather thrilling, being faced with danger on every side."

Her crepe pink silk turban—which matched her too-snug bias-cut rayon gown—practically quivered with excitement. And it must have been doing so for some time, for it had slipped slightly to the side and tufts of her frizzy gray-streaked blonde hair were sticking out. She wore no makeup save a bit of blush pink lipstick and had a large rope of pearls around her neck.

"Oh, yes, it's been quite the...adventure," I said lamely, not sure how else to put it.

"And Mr. deVane has been so kind and considerate about the whole thing. He offered to put us up in a hotel, should we be more comfortable, but of course Mathew wouldn't have it. He wants to be near the action."

"How do you know Mr. deVane?" I doubted the frumpy American had anything to do with spies or robberies, but one never knew.

"Mathew has some sort of business deal going on with him. I've no idea. No head for business whatsoever." She tittered like a schoolgirl, which was odd and awkward and ill-suited on a woman her age. "Harry invited us to stay as we were in England for another of Mathew's little business meetings. Kind of him, don't you think?"

"Oh, yes, very. Is this your first trip to England?"

"Mine, yes, but Mathew has been here, oh, twice before."

Could Mathew Breverman be the spy? Or have something to do with the break-in? Perhaps Harry's study hadn't been tossed because of some government shenanigans. Perhaps it was a simple matter of business competition. Mathew Breverman could have been looking for something to give him a leg up in negotiations or some such.

My mind toyed over various possibilities all through the rest of dinner while Maude prated on about her home, children, and friends back in... somewhere in America. I was a little vague on the matter. Frankly, I wasn't much listening. It was with some relief that we women finally left the table and I was able to get away from Maude.

While the men sucked down their port and cigars, I made a beeline to the drinks cart and gathered all the fixings for an Aviation. Ethel and Amelia Kettington joined me as I was pouring.

"Fix me up one of those, would you," Ethel demanded more than asked. She was wearing an equally out-of-date gown in unrelieved black. It washed her out and made her look even more haggard and horsey than usual.

"Sure thing," I said agreeably, pulling out two more glasses.

"Are you certain Mr. deVane won't mind?" Amelia twittered. Her gown was almost a twin to her sister's but in a ghastly shade of brown which flattered her even less.

"Don't be daft, Amelia. Harry wouldn't leave his liquor lying about if he didn't want us to help ourselves. It's a party, after all."

Ethel might be brusque to the point of rudeness, but she had a point. "Ladies, to your very good health," I said, handing over their drinks.

Ethel took a long draft and let out a gusty sigh of appreciation. "Better than Harry's. You have skills, Lady R."

I ignored the rather familiar moniker. "Please, call me Ophelia."

She used her martini glass to indicate herself first then her sister. "Ethel and Amelia."

"So pleased," murmured Amelia over the rim of her glass.

"Didn't have a chance for a chin wag earlier," Ethel barked.

"No," I said. "We didn't. I take it you're one of Harry's neighbors."

"For years now. Since he bought the place. Glad, too. Was falling to ruin." Ethel slugged back the rest of her drink and held out her glass. "Don't suppose you could mix us up another."

"Of course." While I fixed her another drink, I steered the subject toward the break-in. "I suppose the police questioned you about the break-in last night."

"They did. Ghastly business." Ethel took the drink I held out. "We had nothing to tell them, of course."

"That's not entirely true, sister," Amelia said with a little flutter of her hand. "Remember I heard something during the night?"

Ethel snorted. “She was imagining things, as usual. Vivid dreams. Too much imagination. I pride myself on having no imagination whatsoever.”

“How...lovely for you.” I couldn’t help a slight tinge of sarcasm in my tone, but it appeared to fly over Ethel’s head.

“It does make life simple,” she said proudly. “No getting oneself worked up over nothing.”

“But it wasn’t nothing...” Amelia bit her lip when her sister shook her head.

“Don’t be daft, Amelia. You had a dream. No more.”

Amelia said nothing but stared morosely into her drink. It was clear I needed to get the younger Kettington sister alone if I wanted to discover what she’d heard during the night.

At last the men joined us and Harry clapped his hands to get everyone’s attention. “Ladies and gents,” he said in his smooth, mellifluous voice. “I’ve a treat this evening. A famous jazz musician all the way from the Americas. Hale Davis!”

Everyone clapped politely as Hale appeared in the doorway, bowed, and took his place at the piano. There were oohs and ahhs as he did some complicated scale thing on the piano and everyone settled in comfortably while he trilled out several popular songs such as *St. Louis Blues* and *Mad About The Boy*. Every now and then he’d glance my direction, but it was so quick I wondered if I’d imagined it.

While he played, I caught Aunt Butty up on my investigation so far. Including my confrontation with Binky.

"Don't worry," she assured me. "I've got ways to make that boy talk. When I get done with him, he'll spill all his beans."

"I don't think that's how the saying goes."

She tsked at me and I held back a grin. Aunt Butty had her own way of doing things.

I'd hoped to catch Hale after the evening's entertainment, but Harry hurried him off, and I was left with nothing to do but find my way to bed. I'd downed three Aviations and was definitely feeling well-lubricated. Bed was probably a good idea. I could seek out Hale in the morning.

Once again, Maddie was nowhere to be found, so I undressed myself. I was just pulling on my pajamas when from somewhere in the house below came a bone-chilling scream!

Chapter 10

I dashed into the hallway and nearly crashed into Aunt Butty. We stared at each other a moment. Her hair was up in rags, covered with a silk scarf, and her face was smeared with cold cream. She wore pajamas similar to my own but had managed to throw on feather-tufted mules and a robe whilst I remained barefoot and robe-less.

"You heard that?" I asked.

"Of course. Nearly gave me a heart attack."

"It came from downstairs." Chaz appeared from his room in striped bottoms and a satin smoking jacket.

The three of us charged down the stairs even as other doors opened, and heads popped out. I could hear questioning voices above, but I ignored them, focused on finding the source of the scream.

The marble floor was ice cold against my bare feet as I ran across the foyer and down the hall. The study door stood open for once, light spilling into the hall. A dark figure stood in the doorway, small, angular.

"Maddie? What are you doing here?" I came to a stop beside her and stared into the room.

Sprawled across the rug next to the fire was a man in a cheap, beige suit. Next to him lay a bowler hat as if it had been knocked off his head, perhaps in the midst of a struggle. A knife protruded from the middle of his back and around the knife spread a dark stain.

I turned Maddie to face me. "Don't tell anyone anything. Do you understand?" She stared at me blankly and I gave her a little shake. "Don't speak to anyone but me. This is important, Maddie. Do you understand?"

The urgency in my voice must have gotten to her because she finally nodded. Satisfied, I thrust her at Aunt Butty, and entered the study to kneel beside the body. I reached out and placed my fingers on his neck.

"Should you be doing that?" Chaz asked from the doorway.

"Who else?" At least I had some training in the matter. During the Great War I'd spent some time working as a nurse. Granted, I'd been very junior and had mostly emptied bedpans and cleaned ghastly messes, but I knew a few things about dealing with wounds. And finding pulses. The man on the floor had none.

"Who is he?" Chaz asked, moving closer. "He can't be a guest. Look at that suit. Appalling."

He was right. The cheap wool was scratchy and the cut ill-fitting as if it had been made for a larger man. Plus, the hair—thinning and mousy—was in dire need of a trim. He wasn't anyone from the house party.

I knew I shouldn't touch the body any more than I had to, but curiosity got to me. I carefully turned the man's head, so I could see his face. Even though I'd have expected it, I must have started because Chaz knelt next to me and asked in a low voice, "You recognize him?"

I nodded. "I'll explain later." I turned the dead man's head back into position and climbed to my feet.

A cursory glance around the study revealed nothing out of order, but I didn't have time to investigate properly. More guests had arrived, and voices were shouting in the hall as everyone jostled to see into the room. Harry appeared in the doorway.

"What the deuce is going on?" he all but bellowed.

"I'm afraid we have a bit of a situation," Chaz said calmly, rising to his feet and nodding toward the body.

Harry blanched. "Good god!" He turned and yelled down the hall, "Jarvis! Ring the constabulary!"

"Of course, sir," came Jarvis's voice, as unruffled as ever.

"We should preserve the crime scene for the police," I said quietly as Chaz and I exited the study.

"Is he dead?" Harry asked.

"Afraid so," I replied. "No pulse. And there's a knife through his back."

"Good god," he repeated. His face was ghostly white, and he looked like he might fall over.

"We need to get these people out of here," Chaz said, gripping Harry's arm. "Can't have them in the way. Can you imagine what the ladies will do if they see a body?"

I decided to ignore his denigration against my sex. Instead I focused on searching out Aunty Butty while Chaz and Harry took over, ushering the guests back to bed and closing up the study for the arrival of Detective Inspector Willis.

I noticed Aunt Butty at the top of the stairs. She pointed to her room and disappeared, so I murmured my excuses to Harry, who ignored me, and hurried up to join her.

Maddie was huddled in an armchair next to the fire, unlit on the warm summer night. Aunt Butty sloshed brown liquid into a glass and thrust it at Maddie. "Drink this."

"I-I d-don't drink," Maddie protested. She was shaking like a leaf in a hurricane.

"Tonight, you do," Aunt Butty said firmly, practically forcing the stuff down her throat before tossing some of it back herself. She thrust the bottle to me and I took a heavy swig. The whiskey burned its way down my throat to pool warmly in my belly.

Once Maddie had calmed, I perched on a stool next to her. "Maddie," I said softly, "can you tell me what happened?"

"I was going to return a book I borrowed from the library," she explained, holding up a paperback still clutched tightly in her hand. "So I slipped downstairs after everyone had gone."

"Go on," I encouraged her.

"When I got downstairs, I noticed the light on in the study. I thought maybe Mr. deVane was working late. I was about to turn back when I heard something."

"Heard what?" Aunt Butty asked sharply, taking a seat on the edge of the bed.

"Sounded...like a gurgle?" Maddie frowned.

Maybe the sound of a dying man? "Then what?" I asked.

"Then there was a thud like something fell. And I worried...Mr. deVane is a bit old, ain't he? Maybe he had a fall."

"Old?" Aunt Butty muttered. "I never—"

I hushed her, eager to hear what Maddie had to say next. "So, you decided to help?"

"Yes, m'lady. I pushed the door open all the way. I didn't see Mr. deVane, but I did see that man. He was lying there...and the blood...I think I screamed."

"You did. Rather loudly," Aunt Butty said dryly.

"Sorry, Lady Butty. It did take me for a turn, it did," Maddie said contritely.

For once I didn't bother to correct her form of address. "Did you touch anything?"

"Not a thing, m'lady. I remembered as you once said a crime scene ain't to be touched. And, o' course, that Hercoolees person won't let nobody touch his bodies."

I was fairly certain "that Hercoolees person" was a reference to Agatha Christie's fictional detective, Hercule Poirot. She'd definitely been filching from my library again.

"You did very well, Maddie," I assured her. A thought occurred. "How much time passed between when you saw the body and when you screamed?"

"Oh, right away, m'lady. I was ever so shocked."

I nodded. So, she must have found the body literally moments after the man was killed. "Did you see anyone else in the room? Anyone at all?"

She shook her head. "No, m'lady."

"Curtains moving?"

"No, m'lady. They was open."

And I hadn't noticed any open windows. No way for a killer to escape other than out the door. "No one walked past you in the hall?"

She shook her head vigorously. "I would have seen them."

Damnation. This wasn't looking good for Maddie.

"Alright, Maddie, the police will be here soon, and they'll want to question you."

Her eyes widened. "Why, m'lady? I didn't do nothin'."

"Because you're the one that found the body. Only tell them what you told me, nothing more. Do you understand?"

She nodded, swallowing hard.

"Good. Now go to the kitchen and have the cook make up tea for everyone, including the police. I think it's going to be a rather long night."

She nodded again and scampered from the room. I took her spot in the armchair and liberated the bottle of hooch from Aunt Butty's grasp. I took a long swig and let out a gusty sigh.

"You know something," Aunt Butty said in a rather accusing tone, I thought.

"Not much. But I know who the dead man is."

Her eyes widened. "Who?"

I passed her back the bottle. "I went to the church fete this afternoon and saw a man sneaking about. He looked...I don't know. Out of place. Not to mention he was wearing a bowler hat just like the man who was sneaking around the grounds the other night. So I followed him into the church and saw him in conversation with Binky."

"Binky? In a church?"

"I know. It was odd. They were behaving strangely, like they didn't want anyone to see them talking. I think they were up to something."

"Something nefarious?" she asked with undue excitement.

"Perhaps. I don't know, but when I asked Binky about it, he lied to me. Told me he hadn't talked to anyone."

"And what does all that have to do with the body currently residing in Harry's study?"

I leaned back. "Because the body in Harry's study is the man I saw with Binky."

Unfortunately, I didn't have a chance to confront Binky about the dead man. The minute Willis arrived, he demanded to know who found the body. Naturally, everyone pointed to poor Maddie.

I tried to intervene, but it didn't do a bit of good. After barely listening to her statement, Willis put Maddie under arrest for murder, cuffed her, and sent her off to the police station with Constable Smith.

I did manage to grab a few seconds with her as she was frog-marched to the vehicle. "Remember what I said, Maddie. Don't tell anyone anything. Just ask for a solicitor."

"Can't afford no solicitor."

"But I can. And I will get you the best. I promise. We're going to sort this out."

And then she was gone, the police car racing down the drive and out of sight, spitting gravel in its wake.

"Well, did she listen?" Aunt Butty asked.

"I hope so. I swear, I've never wanted to punch anyone so badly as I want to punch Willis right now."

Aunt Butty gave me a smile reminiscent of a shark. "Don't worry, dear. With a man like that, there are punishments far worse than physical violence."

She had a point. "You mean abject humiliation."

"Indeed."

I lifted a brow. "What did you have in mind?"

"Can you imagine his reaction should the papers reveal it was a pair of *women* who solved this crime and freed an innocent maid from prison?"

"Oh, Aunt Butty, you *are* devious."

"Occasionally," she said with equanimity. "Now let's get dressed, go find that codswallop of a cousin of yours, and get some answers out of him."

That was easier said than done. We scoured the house, but Binky was nowhere to be found. We expanded our search to the grounds, and finally discovered him hiding out in the folly.

The folly of Wit's End had no doubt been built sometime in the Victorian era. It was tucked back in the woods near a small pond and had the oddest distinction of being a perfectly normal round tower, but with a pineapple on top.

"I'm afraid whoever built this folly had eaten too many mushrooms," Aunt Butty murmured as we approached.

"Mushrooms?" I asked.

"Never mind, dear," she said demurely, adjusting her floppy straw hat. It was beribboned and festooned with numerous plumes, making her look like a startled bird.

I always wondered about some of Aunt Butty's escapades. But I shrugged it off. I had other things to focus on.

We trudged up the path and pushed through the door into the folly. There was a single, round room with small slits for windows and a bare, stone floor. Around the room were curved benches and on one of those benches sat Binky, looking terribly forlorn.

"What ho, Binky?" I said chummily.

"Oh, lord, it's you," he groaned.

"You could sound more enthusiastic," I said, plopping on the seat next to him and hoping I wouldn't get smudges all over my lavender dress.

"I couldn't," he said. "I really couldn't."

"Binky, we need to have a talk." Aunt Butty's tone brooked no argument. She spoke to him exactly as a schoolmistress might speak to a naughty child. Binky responded accordingly, sinking low and tucking his head in like a turtle.

"Wasn't me," he said.

"So, you do know about the murder," I said.

He shrugged. "What of it?"

"The dead man in the study is the same man I saw you speaking to at the fete."

"I wasn't speaking to anyone at the fete," he lied, badly.

"Rubbish," Aunt Butty barked. "You were seen. No sense lying about it. Only fools lie about such things. Now who is that man and why is he dead in Harry's study?"

He pressed his lips together. Stubborn man.

"An innocent girl has just been hauled off to jail. If you don't speak up, I shall ensure that you never get another invite anywhere of interest." Aunt Butty glared fiercely at Binky who wilted beneath her gaze.

"Fine, fine. I did speak to that man at the fete, but it was nothing. Just...one of those things. He asked for the time and whatnot. It was nothing."

"You're lying!" I accused.

"Prove it!" He jumped up and stormed out.

"Well," said Aunt Butty, taking his seat. "That went well."

"I was wrong. I want to punch him far more than I want to punch Willis. How am I ever going to get Maddie out of jail if Binky won't tell us the truth?"

"We'll think of something, dear. We always do." Aunt Butty patted my knee.

It was true. We always did. But would we think of it before poor Maddie was convicted and hanged for murder?

Chapter 11

The police station stood near the middle of town, a grim, brick building with a plain facade and an air of gloom. I took the wide steps up and let myself in through the front door. The uniformed officer behind the counter glanced up and gave me a cursory look.

"May I help you, madam?" He said the last word the same way a person might say "tart." And I'm not speaking of the pudding version.

"Lady Rample," I corrected him haughtily. "I would like to see Maddie Crewe."

"I'm sorry, *Lady* Rample, but nobody can speak to prisoners 'cept their solicitors."

"Very well. Has her solicitor been to see her yet?" Aunt Butty had called a friend of hers in London before our foray to the folly. He had assured her that someone would be sent post haste.

"Yes, madam."

I gritted my teeth. "I would like to speak to Detective Inspector Willis."

"He's out, madam." The officer looked down his misshapen nose. It looked like it had been broken in a bar fight. Or perhaps he'd irked his wife one time too many. "Might I take a message?"

"No. Thank you."

I turned around and marched out, practically quivering with annoyance. It's not that I minded people mangling my title. It was his *attitude.* And the fact he wouldn't allow me to see my maid. Poor Maddie must be terrified. But at least the solicitor had been to see her, so that was something. Still, I couldn't rest easy until I'd seen her with my own eyes. What to do?

I knew of only one person who the police might actually listen to. He'd helped me before. Perhaps he would again.

I climbed into my car, revved the engine, and pointed the bonnet in the direction of Fair Woods.

Fair Woods had been in the Varant family since the Norman invasion of England. One of Varant's ancestors had done something noble and been awarded with the land. No doubt the first Varant had built a lovely castle, but what now stood there was a massive Georgian structure, deceptively simple, but brimming with history and wealth.

It was in a marginally better state than Varant's London home, which was a study in shabby gentility. It wasn't that Varant didn't have the money to update things, but rather that he chose to pour his money into his land and businesses. Which made a great deal more sense than dumping a fortune into new carpeting if you ask me.

His butler, Kenworth, greeted me with all the aplomb due my station. I held back a smirk and let him get on about his business. Carrying my card on a silver salver was so last century.

Within minutes Varant had joined me in the parlor and was bending over my hand in a suave and gentlemanly manner. He was handsomely dressed in a simple but elegant gray morning suit that set of his physique nicely. I couldn't help but compare him to Hale.

Both men were equally handsome and well-built. But where Hale was himself without pretense, Varant had a smooth veneer of sophistication that was difficult to penetrate. When it came to women's rights, I'd no idea where Hale stood, but knew that Varant had supported me in my recent endeavors. But would he continue to do so? And did he truly support the equality of women? Or was it just Varant being...polite? Trying to impress me? I'd a feeling there was much about the man I didn't know. May never know.

As for which man was the more proper of the two? Well, that went without saying. Society would always choose Varant. I just wasn't sure I wanted to. Although I did find him decidedly attractive. Not that any of it mattered anyway. As I'd told Hale, I'd no intention of marrying again. And I didn't need to, thanks to dear Felix.

"My lady. What a surprise. Welcome."

"Lord Varant," I said with a smile. "Thank you for seeing me. I know it's rather cheeky popping in like this."

"Peter, please. I am always available for you, Ophelia." The way he said my name sent shivers to intimate places and made me think of very naughty things indeed. Perhaps I wasn't as unaffected by him as I'd like to think.

I cleared my throat. "I could use your help, Peter." It felt strange. I was so used to thinking of him by his title. "I'm in a bit of a sticky wicket, as they say."

"Oh, do tell." He sat down in an armchair across from me and neatly crossed one leg over the other. Before I could so much as open my mouth, Kenworth reappeared with tea and biscuits which he left next to me.

While I poured, I told Varant of the break-in—something he already knew, having received a call from Harry—and the dead man in the study—which he did not. "They've arrested my maid. Ridiculous nonsense."

Varant took a sip of tea. "Why ever would they arrest a maid?"

"She's the one who found the body. I think Willis is cooking up some nonsense about a lover scorned or something. Maddie has no lovers. Certainly not out in the wilderness of Devon."

He gazed at me thoughtfully, expression revealing nothing. "I'm not certain what you want me to do about it."

I bit into a biscuit, hoping I didn't get crumbs down my front. "The police won't let me see her. Maddie. I want you to get me in, so I can talk to her. Make sure she's alright."

"I can probably arrange that." He eyed me carefully. "But there's more to this, isn't there? There's got to be a reason Willis suspects Maddie other than that she found the body."

I cleared my throat. "There would be if he knew about it."

Varant lifted an eyebrow. I noticed he ignored the cookies. Probably why he was so fit.

I sighed. "Maddie was born in Germany."

"And you think with the break in..."

I nodded. "He might think she's a spy, or some ridiculous nonsense. She's not, of course. She's Jewish."

His other brow went up. "Indeed?"

"Her parents left Germany when she was but a babe. She grew up here. She's nearly as English as you or I."

"Well, I'm not sure about that, but she would certainly have no cause to spy for Germany."

"So, there *is* a German spy running amok," I said eagerly. "But why here? Why in Devon?"

He didn't respond, but instead took another sip of tea while looking enigmatic. "I'll have a chat with Willis."

"Thank you." I wanted to prod him more about this spy thing and Neville Chamberlain and his visit to Harry deVane, but the minute I opened my mouth to ask, he interrupted. Unusual for Varant who was a perfect gentleman at all times.

"Thank you for coming, Ophelia, but I must be off. Got to keep this place running." He stood and held out his hand. "I'll have Kenworth give you a ring when I've arranged things with the police."

"Thank you, Varant. Peter. I truly appreciate it." There was nothing I could do but allow him to help me to my feet and show me to the door. But as I walked down the gravel drive toward my car, I was more confused than ever. I had a feeling Varant was hiding something. Something to do with spies.

Chapter 12

The road from Varant's manor to Wit's End passed by the village pub. Just as I approached, a car coming from the opposite direction screeched to a stop outside the pub and Binky climbed out. He was alone and looking a bit frazzled as he entered the pub. I'd no doubt he'd be there awhile, drinking the afternoon away. Which meant this would be the perfect time to search his room.

I accelerated, speeding the rest of the way. By the time I arrived at the manor, I was shaking with nerves, which was silly. Fortunately, I met no one and was able to slip up the back stairs usually reserved for the staff and into Binky's room.

The maids hadn't been in yet and the place was an utter disaster. The bedclothes were in a wad, clothes strewn willy nilly, and the vanity overflowed with jars of pomades and whatnot, some of them tipped on their sides as if he'd been in a hurry.

I'd no idea what I was looking for. Could be anything: a piece of paper with a secret code, a blueprint, a letter. Maybe even a bloody knife. Only that was silly. The knife had been left in the victim's back.

I shook my head at my own wild imagination and began to systematically search the room as best I could. I even got down on my knees to peer under the bed. I rummaged through the rubbish in the waste bin and poked at the empty fireplace. There was a stack of books by the bed which was odd. Binky didn't strike me as much of a reader. But they were all quite innocent and bore nothing of interest.

I finally had to give up. Frustration jabbed at me like a sharp needle. This was getting me nowhere and I was feeling rather overheated and in dire need of a drink. Perhaps there had been something incriminating in Binky's room at one point, but it was certainly gone now.

Rather out of sorts, I stomped down to the drawing room where I was sure to find a beverage of some nature.

I wheedled Mrs. Bates into providing a bowl of ice. Then well-armed, I raided Harry's drinks cupboard for the necessary booze. A few minutes later, I was ensconced in an armchair with a good view of the sweeping lawn, an Aviation in one hand and a book in the other. Not that I could focus on the book. My mind was in far too much of a whirl. But it would be a good excuse to avoid unwanted entanglements of the conversational variety.

Fortunately, the first to put in an appearance was Chaz. "Darling, that looks simply marvelous. How does one make it?"

"Oh, it's terribly easy. Gin, maraschino liquor, lemon juice, and creme de violette."

Chaz followed my instructions, shook it all with ice, and poured it into a delicate martini glass. "Sheer perfection!"

"I should say."

"I can't believe you're not drinking a highball," he said, lounging next to me.

"The Aviation is my new poison."

"Well, if you must have a poison, 'tis a delightful one," he said, sighing over a sip. "How goes the investigation."

"Not well," I admitted. "I haven't been able to get in to see Maddie. Varant's on it."

"Is he."

I ignored his cheek. "I searched Binky's room thoroughly, but there was nothing."

"Dash it all. I was sure Bucktooth Binky was our man!"

"Don't be daft. He's up to something. Of that there's no doubt. And I'm certain it's to do with that man's death. Maddie is innocent."

"Of course, she is. Worst maid ever, but a genuinely decent human."

"Not the worst maid ever," I corrected him. "Just cheeky. Aunt Butty's Flora is the worst maid ever. Calls me 'miss' and can't even brew a decent pot of tea."

"Horrors."

"You'd think so if you ever had to drink it."

We sat in companionable silence for a moment.

"Have you had the chance to spend much time with Hale Davis?" Chaz asked slyly.

"A bit," I admitted.

"I wish it was easier."

"I know."

"I'm surprised Varant agreed to help you. He doesn't particularly like Willis."

I raised a brow. "How do you know?"

Chaz shrugged. "I was in the village and happened to overhear Willis giving Varant the screws."

I leaned forward. "About?"

"His visit here with Chamberlain. The break-in."

"What did Varant say?"

"Not much," Chaz admitted. "Some mumbo jumbo about he and Chamberlain being 'old friends' with Harry and just popping over for a spot of supper. That Chamberlain was 'passing through' and there was nothing at all unusual about it."

"But you don't buy it."

He shook his head. "Not a bit. Varant is an excellent prevaricator, but I've known the man long enough to know when he's beating about the bush, so to speak. There is definitely more to this story."

"Something interesting enough to bring out German spies?" I asked, remembering my chat with Varant.

"No idea. I wouldn't have thought so. Varant is so deadly dull. Well, he is."

"I didn't say anything."

"No, but you were about to defend your darling."

"He isn't my darling," I protested.

"No? What about Hale?"

"I think we've strayed from the topic at hand," I said coolly.

He smirked. "Very well. The point is, Varant was hiding something. Of that there is no doubt. Although Willis seemed to buy his nonsense. More or less. Then again, Willis isn't that bright, if you ask me. But I can't for the life of me figure out how Chamberlain is involved or what German spies have to do with anything."

"Not to mention, who is the man that ended up dead in the study?"

"Yes, there's that, too," he said dryly.

"We're no closer to discovering the truth," I lamented. "And I've no idea where to go from here." I eyed him. "You could cozy up to Binky. Maybe get him to open up."

Chaz made a sound of distaste. "Wonderful. Do I have to?"

"Pretty please? For me."

"If I must. What will you be doing in the meantime?"

"Waiting for Varant to work his magic." And keeping my fingers crossed that we weren't befallen with another disaster.

Feeling a bit anxious and at loose ends, I decided a walk before tea was just the thing. The afternoon sun cast long shadows on the lawn as I stepped outside. It was still warm, but not nearly as chokingly hot as it had been earlier.

A bird chirped sleepily nearby, and the crickets sang their summer tune. The sweet scent of roses teased my nose as I strolled slowly down the garden path beneath trellises and arches toward the river.

It was such a lovely evening that I decided to push the thoughts of murder and mayhem from my mind and enjoy the moment. Bask in the glory of a summer's eve, as it were. There would be plenty of time for maudlin thoughts later.

I caught the stench of a cigarette moments before I rounded a hedge and practically tumbled over a young man sitting on a bench. He wore a chauffeur's uniform and jumped up, red faced, the moment I stumbled upon him.

"My lady! Most sorry." He tried to hide the cigarette, but it was useless. I could see the smoke trailing up from behind his back.

"No worries," I assured him. "We all need a little break from time to time. You're Mr. deVane's chauffeur?" I remembered him from the day Aunt Butty and I had arrived. He'd been the one to hold my door.

"Yes, my lady. Stevens." He tugged at an imaginary cap, his having tumbled to the ground. I doubted sincerely that he was a Stevens. He had a heavy accent of the European variety, though I couldn't quite place it. I suppose it had been muddled by time spent in England.

"As you were, Stevens."

He gave me a wink and a saucy salute, which I let slide. I started to turn away when a thought struck. "Did the police question you, Stevens?"

"About the murder?"

"Or the break-in."

"Yes, my lady. Both. I don't know nothing. Told them so."

"Ah. You sleep over the garage?" Most chauffeurs did in these big houses.

He frowned as if not sure where I was going. "Yes, my lady. Ever since I come to work here."

"Which was?"

His frown deepened.

"When did you come to work for Mr. deVane?"

He squinted up at the sky. "Come now two years ago."

"Ah." He was either very committed to the cause and possibly presentient, or exactly what he said he was. "So, you were in your room the night of the break-in but heard nothing? Saw nothing?"

"No, my lady. I get very tired. Sleep hard. Maybe a little—" He made a tipping motion toward his mouth with one hand.

"Oh, drinking. Yes, that'll do it, I suppose. Same last night?" I needed to know if he had an alibi for the murder

"Last night, go to pub. Have some drinks. Come home. Sleep. Hear nothing. See nothing."

Since the pub closed at eleven, he'd likely been home and in bed before midnight. Which was well before the murder. So, he could have done it. He could also be the spy. He could be lying. But it wouldn't do to accuse him of any of those things. I was suddenly very aware of how alone we were.

"Yes, well, thank you for your help, Stevens. I must be off. Enjoy your smoke." I forced myself to walk slowly as if simply continuing my stroll, but my mind was awash with ideas. Here was a perfect suspect. Why hadn't Willis arrested him? Just because Maddie had found the body...well, that didn't mean anything. I was going to have to dig deeper on this chauffeur. Maybe something ugly would bubble to the surface.

Chapter 13

There was a telephone in the front hall of Wit's End. Tucked into a corner beneath the stairs, complete with a comfortable chair upholstered in red velvet and a curtain for an attempt at privacy. I glanced up and down the hall to ensure I was alone before settling myself in and ringing up Varant. It was getting dangerously close to supper time, but I decided to risk it. This was more important.

Kenworth answered with his usual stiff-upper-lip arrogance. "Fair Woods."

"Hello, Kenworth. Lord Varant, please."

"And who may I say is calling?"

I rolled my eyes. He knew who I was. "Lady Rample, Kenworth. As you well know."

"Very good, my lady. One moment." I heard him put the phone down on the table, then his measured footsteps as he walked away. Slowly. Very slowly. If I could have reached through the telephone and throttled him, I daresay I would have.

I tapped one fingernail impatiently against the telephone table, then inspected it carefully for chips. Same with the rest of my nails. Still all perfectly manicured and painted cream. I generally preferred something brighter. Red or raspberry, but this new color from Revlon had been irresistible. The minute I'd seen it in Selfridges, I'd needed to try it.

Finally, Varant's voice came over the line. "Ophelia?" Clear in his tone was his surprise at my calling him. Not something I usually did. I wasn't sure whether to be put out or not.

"Varant…Peter. At last. I thought Kenworth had disappeared forever."

Varant snorted. "No need to be dramatic." I scowled at his words. I was not being dramatic. "What can I do for you?"

"I was wondering...I know you have contacts in interesting places. If I wanted to check someone's past, how would I go about it?" I asked.

"You mean a background check?"

"That's the one."

There was a pause. "Who do you want checked out?" His tone was resigned.

"Well, there is—"

"Wait! Why don't you send over a list? Have one of Harry's servants drop it off."

I frowned. "Why not just tell you over the phone?"

"Because prying ears might be listening."

I swear I heard an outraged squeak, quickly muffled. Ah, I'd forgotten about small villages. In London, no one would have paid the call any attention, but out here, it would be all over Devon by tea time, thanks to the exchange operators. "Very well. I'll have it sent over straight away. Now about that other matter we discussed. Any movement there?"

"Give it time, Ophelia. The wheels of justice move slowly."

"More like glacially," I muttered.

He chuckled. "I can't guarantee results, but I'll do my best. I'll speak with you later. I've errands to run." And with that he rang off without waiting for me to respond. I wasn't entirely sure whether that was rude or efficient.

Dropping the headset into the cradle I pulled the phone pad toward me and used the pencil provided to scribble a list. At the top was Harry's chauffeur, Stevens. Next, Binky. After all, what did I really know about him? He'd spent no time with Felix, instead gadding about London spending money he didn't have and, as it turned out, never would. I would have liked some information on the dead guy, but since we didn't have a name, that was a lost cause. At least for the moment. Adding "dead guy" to the list would only amuse Varant.

I also included Mathew Breverman simply because he was a stranger and new to the area. I realized, of course, that a woman could just as easily be behind all this, so I added Miss Semple since she was young and reasonably fit and had been at the fete with Binky and me. Not to mention, she was a newcomer to the area, unlike the sisters. For the same reason I included Maude Breverman. Not that I believed she had anything to do with it, but you just never know about people.

I managed to track down Jarvis and beg for an envelope which I proceeded to seal tight. With some reluctance, he sent one of the footmen over to Fair Woods to deliver the list. But only after giving me a few exasperated sighs and some suspicious looks. He reminded me an awfully lot of Varant's butler, Kenworth. Did all butlers train at the same place? Have a rule book which they butled by?

Satisfied that I'd done all I could for now, I ambled into the drawing room for tea. I was rather famished after my endeavors and was pleased to see Mrs. Bates had set out a rather generous spread provided by Cook. There were egg and mango chutney, lobster, and potted shrimp sandwiches, all on thin slices of brown bread. Rose petal sandwiches on soft white bread. Thick slices of Madeira and seed cakes. A plate of brandy snaps. And, naturally, Devonshire splits—scones split in half and stuffed with fresh strawberry jam and clotted cream.

Aunt Butty already had a plate piled high, so I crammed my own plate full and joined her on the settee. I barely waited to sit down before I was stuffing my face.

"That cook does know how to do a proper tea," Aunt Butty said around a mouthful of potted shrimp sandwich.

I nodded happily as I munched on seed cake, almost moaning in delight. I'd ignored the sandwiches entirely in favor of the sweet treats. "That she does."

"Discovered anything new?" Aunt Butty asked in a low voice, glancing around to make sure no one was listening in. They weren't. The sisters were arguing over the merits of Madeira versus seed cake. Binky and Miss

Semple were ignoring the food and instead downing cocktails like there was no tomorrow. Chaz and Harry were both absent—Harry no doubt locked away in his study as usual. And the Breverman's were as busy stuffing their faces as Aunt Butty and I.

"The chauffeur has some kind of European accent," I said. "Could be German."

"I think he's Swedish."

"Swedish? How'd you come up with that?"

"One of the maids. Mary. She's been helping me dress with Maddie gone. She told me he was from Sweden. Or was it Switzerland?" She popped a bite of seed cake in her mouth and chewed thoughtfully.

"Oh, well. I've asked Varant to run a background check on him and a few others."

"You should have him run one on those sisters," she said, nodding toward the two women sitting at a gaming table next to the window. "I don't trust them."

"They've lived in Devon their whole lives. Why would they go about spying for the Germans now?"

"Who knows. Money? People do lots of dastardly things for money. They used to live in this house, you know. Their father had to sell it. Gaming debts. The man he sold it to let it run to ruin and Harry snapped it up for a fraction of the cost. Of course, he poured a great deal into fixing it up."

I glanced at the Kettington sisters' shabby, out-of-date gowns. Probably cost a pretty penny a couple of decades ago, but now they looked like they belonged in a charity bin. "You think they need money that badly? Ethel, the older one, seemed happy enough about Harry fixing the place up."

"Depends. I understand they get a small stipend from what was left of their late father's estate which allows them to live quite modestly, but I imagine it's difficult after having once been so wealthy. No more new clothes. No trips abroad. No lovely foods. No posh manor house. Just the bare bones basics. Not to mention they were once admired and feared in the village, and now..." She shrugged.

"People pity them," I said softly.

She nodded. "Indeed. And Ethel, at the very least, doesn't strike me as a woman who enjoys being pitied."

"No, she doesn't," I agreed.

It was easy for me to imagine what it would be like to be vastly wealthy and lose it all. But in my case, I already knew how to survive without. How to make the most of what one has when one has next to nothing. If I lost everything tomorrow, I would simply carry on. I would manage fine. But the Kettington sisters would have no doubt found it impossible to really adjust to their new circumstances, having never been poor.

I felt suddenly sorry for them. Even if Ethel was a bit of a bully. I could see now how hard things must be for her. A proud woman reduced to such circumstances. No doubt she was doing her best without much help from her rather ditzy sister.

Regardless of circumstances, I found it hard to imagine either of them murdering a random stranger in their neighbor's study. Miss Semple on the other hand...

I eyeballed the woman in question. She was flirting wildly with Binky, who seemed flattered. Chaz was still nowhere to be seen. Harry had appeared from the depths of his study and was deep in conversation with Mathew Breverman, so I guess there weren't many other options for her. Could she have been the one to strike the deadly blow?

I couldn't imagine why. Unless, perhaps, the victim knew something about her. Something that might hinder her marriage machinations. And she had been at the fete, though I hadn't seen her anywhere near the stranger. Maybe she was helping Binky with whatever he was up to. Or maybe she was entirely innocent, and Binky had been using her as cover. I found it difficult to credit him with such intelligence, but then again, stupidity would make a perfect cover for a spy.

I spent the rest of the afternoon in my room writing up notes about the murder and break-in. I needed to get my thoughts in order and writing them out helped. If I was a betting woman, I'd say the break-in and murder were connected. In fact, the victim was likely the initial criminal returning to the scene after having been unsuccessful in his first attempt—regardless of what Constable Smith had claimed. It would make perfect sense. In fact, it was the only thing that did. But the facts remained:

Why had he broken in?

What was he after?

Who had killed him? (After all, Harry deVane or his employees would have had a perfect right to kill an intruder. No one would have blamed them, so why not confess?)

And, perhaps most importantly, who was the man? And was he the spy I'd heard Harry, Chamberlain, and Varant talking about that first night after supper?

It made perfect sense to me that he was, indeed, the spy. That he'd broken in to steal...something. He'd failed the first time—or at least partially failed, perhaps not obtaining all the information necessary—and so broken in again. But this time someone had been ready for him. With a knife.

But why the secrecy? A simple cover story would be that the man was a robber and the killer had simply been defending himself, or herself. That would be the end of it, no one the wiser as to the true motives. Unless...

The dead man wasn't the spy at all but had been called there by someone. To meet the real spy, perhaps? Why? Because the man knew the identity of the spy and had threatened to tell? Or perhaps he was simply a loose thread that needed tying and the spy had done away with him in order to keep his, or her, secret. It made sense. But that begged the question—

A soft knock at the door interrupted my thoughts.

"Who is it?"

I assumed it was Aunt Butty, or perhaps Chaz, but no one replied. Instead, there was a faint scraping sound as an envelope was slid under the door.

I got up quickly and dashed across the room, throwing open the door. The hall was empty. No one in sight. How bizarre.

I shut the door and collected the envelope. It was thick and creamy, and my name was scrawled across the front in black ink. It matched the stationary that I'd been provided in my room. No doubt every guest had access to it.

I slit the envelope with a silver letter opener from the desk and pulled out a single sheet of paper. In the same sprawling hand was the message: *Meet me in the rose garden before supper.* It was signed with Hale's name.

My heart gave a little flutter of excitement. We hadn't had much of a chance to speak since the walk to the fete.

I glanced at the time. It was still a good hour until the evening meal, so I rushed my toilette. And, with thirty minutes to spare, descended the stairs. The drawing room was empty, so I stepped out through the French doors leading to the great lawn. A path took me 'round to the rose garden at the side of the house in front of the long, low orangery building.

The roses perfumed the dusky evening with their heady scent, inviting me to relax and enjoy a leisurely stroll, but I was too eager. I strode briskly down the path, assuming Hale meant to meet me at one of the benches tucked beneath the trellises. It was all rather mysterious and romantic.

The little flutter grew stronger. It was ridiculous, reacting to a man like this. I was a modern woman, in control of her emotions. Aunt Butty would no doubt laugh and tell me there was no such thing as being in control of emotions when it came to men. Such feelings were meant to be enjoyed, savored, and experienced.

Unfortunately, the rose garden was empty. Perhaps I was early. I sat down on the first bench, folding my hands genteelly in my lap, trying not to fidget. The perfume of roses teased my nose, along with something else. Something slightly sweet. Vanilla? Almond? How odd.

One moment I was sitting there, enjoying the evening. The next, something was wrapped around my neck and someone was choking the life out of me!

Unable to scream, I writhed against my attacker, jamming my fingers up beneath the scrap of material around my throat, trying to pull it away. I kicked wildly, using my body weight to thrust myself forward, then back, slamming into my attacker.

The move was unexpected, causing the attacker to stagger and the noose to go slightly slack. I dragged in a lungful of air and let out an unholy shriek. Startled, the attacker let loose the bit of fabric—which fluttered to the ground—whirled and ran. I tried to get a good look, but he—I assumed it was a man—had disappeared into the bushes.

"It came from here!" Aunt Butty's strident voice echoed over the gardens.

"I heard it, too." Miss Semple, not to be left out.

"Down here." Chaz, taking charge.

Footsteps crunched on the gravel as the entire guest list charged down the path toward me. They stopped abruptly as they spotted me.

"Ophelia," Aunt Butty cried. "Are you all right?"

I shook my head. "Someone just tried to kill me."

Chapter 14

While Harry and Chaz led a search of the gardens, the Misses Kettington returned to the house to telephone the police. Aunt Butty inspected me for injuries. Assured I was alright, she bent down to scoop up the bit of pink and white striped fabric from the ground.

She held it out to me. "Isn't this your scarf, Ophelia?"

I stared at it in horror before plucking it from her outstretched hand. "Yes," I said, my voice husky.

"You're going to have one almighty bruise," she proclaimed before ushering myself, Maude, and Miss Semple back to the house.

I touched my throat which already felt raw and sore. "They used my own scarf; can you believe it?"

"You're sure you didn't see who it was?" Miss Semple asked, eyes wide. I thought she looked a little paler than usual, but it was hard to tell.

I eyed her closely, but she showed no signs of being in on it. She looked rather shocked and genuinely concerned.

"I'm afraid not. It was so sudden and he, or she, was behind me. Then when I managed to get loose, the attacker ran off into the bushes. Didn't even get a glimpse."

"Harry will find him," she assured me.

I wasn't so sure.

At that moment, Hale came charging down the path. He stumbled to a halt when he saw me surrounded by the other female houseguests.

"Sorry, heard a scream," he said lamely, glancing from me to the other women. He clearly didn't want them thinking this was anything personal.

"Lady Rample was attacked," Mrs. Breverman said breathlessly.

"Good god!" Hale exclaimed. He looked like he wanted to say more, do more, but he restrained himself.

"Run ahead and have Jarvis pour a brandy. And tell Mrs. Bates to stoke the fires," Miss Semple ordered as if he was just another servant.

"No fire," I protested. "The night is warm enough as it is. I will take that brandy, though."

A ghost of a smile quirked Hale's lips. "Consider it done."

"Well? What are you waiting for?" Miss Semple demanded. "Run along."

I shot her a dirty look, but Hale merely tugged on an imaginary forelock and said, "Yes'm, right away." With a wink at me, he turned and strode back up the path toward the house.

Miss Semple, meanwhile, clutched at her pearls. "Well, I never."

"Mr. Davis is not a servant, Miss Semple," Aunt Butty said severely. "He's a musician." As if that settled it, she took my arm. "Now, come. Ophelia has had such a shock. We must see her to the house." She charged up the path behind Hale with me in tow, the other women trailing along behind us. For once, Julia Semple was speechless.

Once back in the drawing room, ensconced in a comfortable armchair and with brandy in hand, I was able to take stock. Someone had tried to murder me! I had assumed the note was from Hale. It was signed by him, after all. But what if it wasn't? Because I wouldn't believe for a moment that Hale had lured me into the garden to choke me to death. Still, I'd have to ask him about the note. Later. When Miss Semple wasn't eyeballing me with great suspicion. I did not need tongues wagging about me and Hale. Not that I much cared what society thought of me, but I did care what it thought of Hale. Because he had neither money nor position to protect him from gossiping tongues.

Shortly after I'd finished the brandy, Chaz and the other men returned. "Nothing," he admitted wryly. "Bas—er, he got away. Too much of a lead, I'm afraid."

I wanted to swear a blue streak. Instead I said, "Dash it. No clue at all?"

He dropped into the seat next to me. "There was one thing," he said in a low voice. He held out his hand. In his palm was a button. A plain little thing. Brass, no sort of decoration of any kind. "Found it in the bushes. Had to have been recently dropped. Figured it got torn off his jacket or something."

I took it from him, turning it between my fingers. "I don't recognize it. Could be from anything."

He shrugged. "It's all I found. I didn't tell the others because..."

"Surely none of them could have done it. Weren't they all inside?" They'd all come down the path with him, I was fairly certain.

"I was in my room when I heard you scream. Took a bit to get downstairs. By then, Harry and Mathew were already in the drawing room with the female guests. Binky joined us at some point, not sure when. He might have been in the room already. Couldn't swear to it."

"So how could any of them have attacked me?"

"I don't think they could have. But there are the servants. And Hale Davis."

"Hale wouldn't hurt me."

He lifted a brow. "You sure?"

"Yes." And I was. There were a lot of things in life I was unsure about, including Hale's intentions. But I was absolutely certain of the fact he would never harm me. Nor would Chaz. And I wasn't sure a woman would be strong enough. That left Harry, Mathew, and the servants. "But there is the chauffeur." I told Chaz about asking Varant to check on the chauffeur's background, as well as that of the others. "Maybe someone overheard me."

"It's possible. And a brass button could have come from a chauffeur's uniform. We're going to have to find a way to search his rooms."

"I'm all for that, but not tonight."

Just then Jarvis arrived in the drawing room with Willis who immediately charged over to me. "I hear someone tried to wring your neck."

"Not exactly elegantly put, Detective Inspector, but accurate nonetheless."

"What happened?" He shooed Chaz away and took his spot. Chaz let him, looking amused.

I told Willis about going into the garden, sitting on the bench, but I left out the part about the note. "Next thing I know there's scarf around my neck and someone's trying to choke the life out of me."

"Why were you in the garden, Lady Rample?"

"It was warm. I wanted some fresh air," I lied.

He gave me a look rife with suspicion. "That all?"

"What other reason could there be?"

He harrumphed. "Why would someone want to kill you?"

"I've no idea. Isn't it your job to find out?" I wasn't about to tell him it was likely because I was snooping in his investigation.

"That's what I'm trying to do," he said crossly. "Do you have any enemies?"

"None, unless you count my husband's cousin, Lord Rample."

Willis tugged at his ear and glanced across the room at Binky who currently hovered near the drinks cart. "Alphonse Flanders? That Lord Rample?"

"We call him Binky, but yes. He's rather jealous that I inherited my husband's money. All he got was the title and the entailed estate. He's rather bitter about it, but I can't see him trying to strangle me over it."

"Maybe he wants the money."

"Except he doesn't get it and he knows it. Everything goes to my Aunt, should she outlive me."

"And if she doesn't?" he asked

I frowned. "That's getting rather personal, isn't it?"

"I'm trying to solve an attempted murder here, Lady Rample. Yours."

"Fair point. If I outlive her, there are a number of charities that benefit. I doubt any of them would send an assassin after me."

He smirked. "You've quite an imagination, my lady."

"I try."

"So, there's nothing you can tell me about your attacker?"

"Nothing at all," I admitted. "Not even if it was male or female. Thought I'm guessing male, based on strength alone. Still, with the right leverage..."

He nodded. "Could have been a strong woman."

"Exactly. Now, if you'll excuse me Inspector, I feel in need of a lie down."

I didn't, of course, need a lie down. I'm made of sterner stuff than that, but I wanted to get away from Detective Inspector Willis and the others. I needed room to think. And I wanted to talk to Hale.

Fortunately, I found him lounging in a dark corner just outside my room. "Hale."

"Ophelia." His kiss was warm, unhurried, as his hands roamed down my back as if making sure I was in one piece.

I pulled away and dragged him into my room before someone caught us necking in the corridor. I felt suddenly like a naughty schoolgirl.

"Are you alright?" he asked the minute the door was closed.

I touched my throat. "I'll have a bruise, no doubt, but otherwise I'm fine."

"I'm sorry I was late. If I'd been there..."

"So, you *did* send the note."

"Of course. Paid one of the maids to slide it under the door." He sank down onto the chaise longue and pulled me on top of him. It was a rather inelegant position, but I was not averse. "I wanted to see you again. We've barely had a moment alone. But I was waylaid by Jarvis."

"What did he want?"

"To give me instructions about the party this weekend."

"Oh."

"If I'd been there—"

"If you'd been there, he might have tried to kill you, too."

"I'd like to see him try," he said grimly.

"I prefer you alive and unharmed."

His eyes twinkled naughtily. "Oh, do you?"

Sometime later I came up for air. "Only now we've got a problem."

Hale blinked. "What?" His tone was one of utter confusion. Not that I blamed him. He'd no idea how many different things my mind could focus on at once.

"How did the killer, or attempted killer, know that you'd given me that note or that you'd be late?"

He shrugged, coming around remarkably. "Maybe he didn't. Maybe he simply followed you, saw an opportunity."

"But he came armed with a scarf. *My* scarf."

Hale nodded thoughtfully. "When did you last see that particular scarf?"

I pondered a moment, recalling my foray into the cellar and the quick change after. "The day after the break-in. I had it with me at lunch. We dined on the lawn. I think I must have left it on the table or something, because it was quite warm. I think I remember taking it off, putting it down, but I don't recall having it when I went upstairs later."

"So, maybe your attacker grabbed it then."

"But why?"

"Perhaps he planned to return it but never got 'round to it."

A thought sparked. "Or maybe he was going to use it to frame me for something!"

"Always a possibility, I suppose. Now can we not talk about murder and mayhem for a moment?"

I lifted a brow. "Only a moment?"

Chapter 15

The next morning as I drank my tea and nibbled on toast—brought to me by Mrs. Bates since Maddie was otherwise occupied—I made a list of clues about my attacker. There was precious little.

1. Button, brass, plain
2. Scarf, mine, lost?
3. Scent, sweet, vanilla? almonds?

And that was it. There'd been no voice, no visual. No dropped driving license or letter with the attacker's name conveniently written on it. The only thing left was to go through the clues one by one.

The button could have come from the chauffeur's uniform. It looked like the sort of thing to be found on a uniform. I'd have to see if I could sneak in and have a look at his jackets. But, frankly, it could have come from anyone's clothing. Chaz had a nautical blazer, and I didn't doubt at least one of the other men did, too. Nautical was all the rage these days. Aunt Butty had a hat decked out in red, white, and blue ribbons and rosettes, loaded down with brass buttons.

My scarf I was fairly sure I'd left in the garden after luncheon the day after the break-in. Again, anyone could have picked it up and kept it. Either they didn't realize who it belonged to, and therefore weren't sure who to return it to, or they did know and either forgot or kept it for nefarious purposes. Either way, it didn't narrow things down except, perhaps, to people in the house: guests and staff. And Harry, of course. It also ruled out Varant and Neville Chamberlain since neither of them had been there. Although I couldn't imagine why the former would try and murder me, and the latter was no doubt long gone back to London.

Finally, that sweet scent. I couldn't place it other than it smelled like...biscuits. Or cake perhaps. Unfortunately, it didn't clue me in to my attacker. No one smelled like that. Although I supposed I hadn't sniffed everyone thoroughly. It wasn't any sort of perfume I was familiar with. Could it be Cook or her assistant? Could they be in on it? Or could the attacker have had a pocket full of biscuits?

I laughed at my own nonsensical ideas. This was getting nowhere fast.

Really, there was little I could do other than attempt a visit with Maddie, check the chauffeur's uniforms, and go around sniffing people. Which would no doubt make me look like a lunatic. But there was nothing for it if I wanted to discover the truth.

Tucking my notes away, I finished my toilette with a swipe of lipstick and a string of Tahitian pearls and exited my room.

While I was breakfasting, Jarvis delivered me a note. It was from Varant. He'd had a word with Willis's superiors, and I was to be allowed to visit Maddie any time I wished. Huzzah! Take that Willis!

The minute breakfast was over, I took my car into town and marched into the police station. I'd barely opened my mouth to demand to see my maid when the desk sergeant gave me a supercilious smile.

"Lady Rample. Detective Inspector Willis said to expect you. This way, please."

I felt like grumbling but held my tongue. I hadn't expected it to be this easy, even with Varant's clout behind it. I suppose I should have known better.

The sergeant led me to a small room with a couple of chairs on either side of a narrow table. The floor was scuffed, the lightbulb dim, and the walls a depressing green that verged on gray. The single window overlooking the street was in desperate need of a wash, the fine film of dust partially blocking the morning light. The place stank of stale cigarettes and old tea.

Maddie sat at the table looking tired and pale, but otherwise none the worse for wear. She looked up and, seeing me, appeared suddenly hopeful.

"M'lady!" She jumped to her feet, hands clasped to her flat chest.

"Sit down. Sit down." I waved at her as I took my own seat. I'd give anything for a cup of strong tea, but based on the odor, I decided to wait. "How are you doing, Maddie?"

She grimaced. "Been better. Could be worse."

"Have you seen your solicitor?"

"Yes, m'lady. He was in the other day. I can't thank you enough for sending him."

"I am not about to allow this Willis person to railroad you into a confession."

"Wouldn't do it no how," she said, her jaw set into stubborn lines.

I had no doubt of it. "Good girl. What did the solicitor say?"

"Mr. Jones said it's poppycock. They've no evidence and no right to hold me. He said I'll be out by the end of the day." She didn't look convinced.

"If that's what he says, then you should believe him. He's one of the best." I studied her closely. "Maddie, do you recall the scarf I was wearing the afternoon after the break-in? The one with pink and white stripes."

"Of course, m'lady."

"Do you remember if I was wearing it when I came up to get ready for supper later that day?"

She scrunched up her face in thought. "No, my lady, you weren't. Fact, I went down to find it thinking you must 'ave left it somewhere. I even checked the garden."

"Did you find it?"

"No. Somebody picked it up." She frowned. "I think it was that Binky person."

My eyebrows went up at that. "Binky took my scarf?"

"I'm almost certain of it. When I stepped out on the terrace, he was standing next to the table. When he heard me, he turned around and looked all guilty. He was holding something in his hand, all scrunched up like. I asked had he seen your scarf and he barked at me like I was an idiot and walked away. I thought on it, and I'm pretty sure that's what he was holding. But I couldn't very well tell on him. Who'd believe me against a lord?"

She had a point. "You could have told me."

She shrugged. "I was gonna get Mary, that's the maid as cleans his room, to poke around for it. But before I could ask, that whole thing with the dead guy happened. Who was he?"

"We still don't know, I'm afraid." Even to my maid I wasn't going to mention the fact I'd seen the dead man with Binky. But I did think it was an interesting coincidence that Binky had also likely taken my scarf.

After assuring myself that Maddie was well, I exited the police station, my mind spinning. Binky had shown up at a party in the middle of nowhere where he knew no one and proceeded to have a secret meeting with a man who later turned up dead. Binky had also likely taken my scarf which was later used in an attempt to strangle me. Yes, Binky and I needed to have a conversation. And this time I was bringing in the big guns.

As I pulled into the drive at Wit's End, I passed Harry's Bentley pulling out, the chauffeur at the wheel and Harry in the back, nose in a paper. I smiled to myself.

This was the perfect time to search the chauffeur's quarters.

Instead of pulling up to the front door, I drove around to the garage. No one was in sight, so I slipped inside and took the stairs to the upper floor where the chauffeur's apartment was. The door was unlocked so I stepped inside and took stock.

It was one large room tucked up under the eaves of the garage. To my left was a tiny kitchenette with a cooker barely big enough to boil a kettle on. To the side of that was a small sink above which hung a rack for dishes and cups. On the other side was a curtained area which I assumed held the loo.

Straight ahead was a table big enough for two, tucked up under a low window. On either side were rickety chairs. They looked like antiques and had no doubt come from the big house at some point. Probably Harry had ditched them when he was renovating. In the center of the room on a round braided rug was a single armchair and next to it a stand which held a lamp and a radio.

To the right, in the darkest corner, was a narrow bed and next to it a single door wardrobe made of cheap pinewood.

"Eureka," I muttered to myself.

I threw open the door of the wardrobe. In addition to regular clothing, a single chauffeur's uniform hung neatly. Obviously, he was wearing the other, so I couldn't check that, but I doubted he'd be wearing a uniform with a missing button. I checked the spare. The brass buttons were similar to the one Chaz had found, but the spare uniform had all its buttons. Dash it all.

I checked the hamper and found nothing but a handful of dirty linens and shirts. So, unless he was running around in a uniform that was missing a button, the chauffeur was out. It had been too easy anyway.

I returned to the house, more convinced than ever that Binky held the clues to all of this. I needed to confront him once and for all, but I was going to need help.

I found Aunt Butty in the morning room, sipping tea, and reading a rather torrid romance novel. I made a mental note to borrow it at some point in the future.

"Ophelia," she exclaimed when I entered. "How is poor Maddie?"

"Holding up." I quickly told her what I'd discovered and outlined my plan.

She smiled smugly and set aside her novel. "Oh, this should be fun. Lead on!"

Chapter 16

Binky was at one of the tables in the garden sipping what looked like lemonade. I was betting there was something stronger in it. Binky didn't strike me as the lemonade sipping type.

Aunt Butty took a seat to his left. I sat on his right. Binky glanced askance from one to the other of us. "What are you two up to?" His tone was rife with suspicion.

"We need to have a discussion, nephew."

He sneered at Aunt Butty. "You are no relation of mine."

"But you are a relation of Ophelia's—if only by marriage—and therefore, you are unfortunately a part of my family."

He blinked, her logic clearly confusing him. Finally, he sighed heavily and with no little exasperation. "What do you want?"

"We know you tried to kill me," I said.

His mouth dropped opened. "What the deuce?" His surprised seemed genuine. "Why ever would I do that?"

"To get your hands on my money."

"As if that's even a possibility," he scoffed. "I've no doubt you've left it to your aunt. Or some home for wayward cats."

"You're not wrong there," I said calmly. "Still, we know you did it."

"I did not! This is ridiculous. What makes you think I would do such a thing?"

"Besides the fact you're jealous of me?" I asked. "How about you stole my scarf. The scarf that was used to strangle me."

He sputtered a little, and finally managed. "Did not."

We both stared at him, silent. He fidgeted. Aunt Butty leaned toward him a little. He nearly fell out of his chair.

"All right. I took it. I admit it. It was just lying there on the divan and I thought...well, maybe it would come in useful."

"For what?" I asked, curious.

He shrugged. "I, ah, don't know. But the point is, I didn't try and kill you. Because the very next night, it was gone from my room. I assumed one of the maids stole it."

I glanced at Aunt Butty. "What do you think?"

"I'm afraid he's telling the truth. Or at least part of it." She leaned even closer to Binky, her eyes narrowing. "Why would you need Ophelia's scarf? What use could you have for it? Let me guess...you were going to frame her for that man's murder!"

He looked a little stunned. "Why ever would I do that? I didn't kill him. Why would I kill him?" His voice had gone squeaky.

"Because," she said, giving him a sly smile, "you were spying for him."

"You've no proof," he spluttered.

Which, of course, was all the proof we needed. Butty leaned back, crowing in triumph. "So, you *are* a spy!"

"It's not...it's not spying," he hissed. "And lower your voice."

"What is it, then?" I asked.

He rubbed his forehead. "Look, I'm in a rather precarious position thanks to my cousin Felix. I've got this massive estate. Total money pit, but I can't get rid of it. There are ways to maybe turn a profit with it, but I need money to fix it up. See?"

I was impressed that he had even gone to the trouble of figuring out a way to make the estate work rather than letting it rot. He'd never shown an ounce of initiative before. Otherwise Felix might have left him some money.

"Go on," Aunt Butty urged.

"Well, I went to the banks, but it was a no go. None of my so-called friends would help, either. I thought it was a lost cause when I was contacted by this man."

"The dead one?" I asked. "The one you were talking to in the church on the day of the fete?"

He nodded. "His name is Barker. He told me he could help. I laughed at him, of course. I mean, he wasn't of *our* class, was he?"

I ignored the bigoted attitude and urged him to continue.

"Barker said he represented someone who had need of certain...information. A businessman who wanted to compete for government contracts, that sort of thing. If I could get this information, then he would give me what I needed for the estate." Binky rubbed a hand through his thinning hair. "By this point, I was desperate. And I figured there was no harm in it. What would it hurt if this man got the government contracts instead of some other chump?"

"Binky, you are an idiot. That man wasn't working for some contractor. He was a foreign spy." I had zero proof of that, but I was hazarding a wild guess based on equally wild conjecture.

He went sheet white. "Why would you say that? It's not…it can't be true."

"We have our methods," Aunt Butty said. "Why would you do such a stupid thing, Binky?"

He tugged at his hair. "I was in too deep. There was nothing else I could do. And you can't tell anyone. They'll hang me for treason."

"No doubt," Aunt Butty said dryly. "It *is* treason."

"But I didn't know!" he all but wailed. "How could I have known?"

"Maybe you should have tried not spying in the first place," I snapped. "What was the meeting in the church about?"

He looked miserable. "I was sent here to gather information from the meeting between Harry deVane and Neville Chamberlain. Only when I went to deliver it, I decided enough was enough. I told Barker I was done. Lied and said someone knew about me. I thought he'd let me go if they thought I was compromised."

"But they didn't," I mused.

He shook his head. "Barker threatened me. I didn't know what else to do!"

"So you lured your contact to the manor and murdered him," Aunt Butty said.

"No! No, I did not. I was...I was going to turn myself in. Tell Harry or Varant or somebody. Hope they threw me in prison or something instead of hanging me." He leaned his elbows on the table and rested his face in his hands. "I didn't know what else to do. And then my contact—Barker—turned up dead in Harry's study. I knew then I couldn't tell anybody. They'd think I'd killed him."

"What was your contact doing at Wit's End?" I asked.

He shook his head. "No idea. I assume he was going to harm me. Or maybe he was trying to find more information on Harry and Chamberlain's dealings."

I tapped my lower lip. "And the break in? Were you behind that?"

"Of course. I stole the papers that Chamberlain had brought to Harry. But I couldn't just take them, I had to make it look like it was an outside job. So I staged the break in."

"What was in them?" Aunt Butty asked.

He shook his head. "No idea. They were sealed in a manila envelope."

"And the man who hired Barker in the first place?" I asked. "Your real employer, who is he?"

"I don't know." He tugged at his tie as if it was suddenly strangling him. "Barker never told me. Just called him 'our friend' or 'Mr. X.'"

"Did he say anything else about Mr. X?" I asked. "Anything at all? Anything that might clue us in to his identity."

"No. No. Just 'our friend, Mr. X.' And that Mr. X was close by, watching." He shuddered.

"What about the documents you burned in the fireplace?" I asked.

He blinked. "What documents? I didn't burn anything. Just grabbed the envelope, broke the window, and ran."

It totally made sense. I turned to Aunt Butty. "Do you believe him?"

"Yes, actually."

Binky let out a shuddered sigh of relief. "Now what? Are you going to turn me in?"

"No, I think not," Aunt Butty said. "You know what you did was wrong, and you won't do it again. Will you?"

He shook his head vigorously. "Of course not."

Her smile was sly. "Good. And one of these days, I'm going to have a use for you."

Binky paled.

With Binky out of the frame as either the killer or my attacker, I felt like we were nearly back to square one. Nearly. Somebody had still lost a button. Someone had still stolen my scarf from Binky. Someone who smelled like baked goods.

What I needed was some thinking time. And a good, stiff drink.

I returned to the house and the drawing room where I knew Harry kept the alcohol. Or at least enough I could make myself a beverage.

I found Amelia Kettington sitting next to the window, placidly knitting. Her needles clacked gently as the green wool turned into something else like magic. It looked like a scarf or shawl.

I helped myself to the drinks cart, quickly whipping up my new favorite cocktail, before strolling over to Amelia. I hadn't much spoken to the youngest Kettington sister and thought now might be a good time. Maybe something would shake loose while my mind was on the inane. I had intended to ask her about what she'd overheard the night of the break-in, but it was no longer important, seeing as we knew Binky was behind it. "May I join you?"

She glanced up, peering at me over her little half-moon glasses. "But of course, Lady Rample."

"Ophelia, please."

She smiled. "Right. Ophelia. Such a lovely name."

"Thank you," I said, taking a seat. "What are you making?"

"A blanket for my cousin's new grandson. I do so enjoy making things. Don't you?"

"Ah, I'm not much for handicrafts," I admitted. "I'm all thumbs. Though I greatly admire those with the skills for it."

She smiled beneficently. "Well, we can't all be so talented."

"I understand you grew up here. At Wit's End."

She glanced around looking a little sad. "Yes, indeed. Although it was called Twin Oaks back then. Father sold it when I was a young woman, you see. We simply couldn't keep up with it. Too much expense. It was the smart thing to sell."

"It must have been hard though."

"It was very difficult," she admitted. "More so for Ethel. I think she felt that by losing our home, we lost our place in society, as well."

"Is that true?"

She pursed her lips thoughtfully. "I suppose it is, in part. We are no longer the 'ladies of the manor' so to speak. It's Harry who is asked to open fetes and cut ribbons and that nonsense. I don't mind. I'd rather be home. But Ethel...she feels the slight very keenly, I'm afraid."

I drained my cocktail and set it aside, suddenly realizing the sweet scent that had been teasing my nose wasn't entirely from the drink. And it was a scent I recognized. "I'm sorry, are you wearing perfume?"

She seemed a bit startled by my intimate question. Then she laughed. "Oh, no, dear. I never wear the stuff. It's a liniment. Works wonders for arthritis and such." She held up a hand, the knuckles a little thick. "My hands were a little stiff this morning, so I borrowed some from Ethel. Smells delightful doesn't it? Vanilla so it doesn't smell so...medicinal."

"The ointment is your sister's?"

"Yes, dear. She uses it all the time."

Suddenly, everything clicked into place. "Excuse me, will you, Amelia?"

"Of course, dear," she said gently. "I suppose you need to get ready for the party tonight."

"Oh, is that this evening?" I'd completely lost track of time.

"Yes, dear. The guests will be arriving any minute. It'll be just like old times." Her face glowed with happiness.

"Yes, of course," I murmured. But I wasn't listening. I was thinking furiously. I knew who the killer was.

Chapter 17

There was no time to wait for Aunt Butty, Chaz, or anyone else. Time was of the essence. What if she tried to kill again? I had to stop her.

I searched the entire house, unable to find my quarry anywhere. Scouring the gardens produced similar results, until, at last, I found her down near the reflecting pool feeding the swans. Sure enough, I realized as I stepped close that she smelled just like my attacker had. Vanilla, and what I realized now was likely mint.

"Hello, Ethel."

She turned her head, her long, horsey face creased in a scowl. "It's Miss Kettington to you."

"Then it's Lady Rample to you."

She snorted. "Just because you married above your station, doesn't mean you are one of us. Despite my lack of title, breeding will tell."

"Ah, then I suppose I should mention my maternal grandfather was an Earl." Technically, it was my great-grandfather, but I decided she didn't need to know that.

Her startled expression gave me a thrill. "How is that...never mind. It doesn't matter. Please leave me be. I wish to be alone."

"I don't think so. You see, I know what you did and why you did it."

Her eyes widened. "Pardon?" Her tone was haughty, her nose tilted ever so slightly up.

"You hated that you lost your home to someone like Harry deVane. Someone with no title or family. Someone so far beneath you. And yet, here he was, living the high life in your home while you struggled to make ends meet in some ghastly cottage in the village where those who once kowtowed now stare at you in pity."

Her face flushed an angry, mottled red. "What of it?"

"It isn't fair, is it?"

"Of course not," she snapped. "Nothing I can do about it." She threw a bit of bread rather viciously and it bounced off a swan's head. The bird let out an angry squawk, flapping its wings.

"But you could," I said. "If you have the money."

"But I don't."

"You don't now, but you had a plan to get it."

She gave me a look like she thought I was a crazy person. "And how, exactly, was I going to do that?"

"A man approached you. He wanted information and he thought you could get it. If you did, he would give you enough money to buy back this place. And so, you became a spy."

Her braying laugh echoed across the pool. "What a lot of stuff and nonsense. As if I would ever spy for anyone."

"You were ordered to collect some information from Harry deVane, so you wangled an invitation to his house party. He felt bad for you, so he went along with it.

Once you were in, you thought you had it made, until someone broke in and stole the information first."

"You're mad!"

"Afraid your contact would be angry, you lured him here to Wit's End and killed him. And then you tried to kill me when you thought I was too close to the truth."

She snorted. "You have lost your mind."

This wasn't going at all to plan. "I have proof."

She crossed her arms. "Show me then."

"The liniment you wear. I smelled it the night I was attacked. My attacker was wearing it just as you are wearing it now. It was you who tried to strangle me."

She shrugged. "What of it? I may use it occasionally, but it's my sister who makes it. It proves nothing."

"It proves she needs to be silenced," a new voice broke in.

We both whirled to find Amelia Kettington standing behind us, the expression on her face slightly mad.

"Whatever are you going on about, Amelia?" Ethel snapped.

"She knows." Amelia pointed at me. "She must be stopped."

She charged toward me. I was so astonished by her speed, I hadn't time to brace myself or get out of the way. Before I could so much as bat an eyelash, she shoved me, and I went flying back into the water.

I landed hard, my head submerged, water surging into mouth and nostrils. I pushed up gasping for air, but Amelia was on top of me. She shoved my head down, forcing me below water again. I clawed at her, surprised by her strength as she wrapped her hands around my throat. I held my breath, desperately struggling against her. The edges of my vision went black. This was it.

And then she was gone, and I was up choking and trying to suck in air. I squinted against the water in my eyes to find Ethel Kettington with her arms around her sister's waist, desperately trying to restrain her. I wasn't sure she'd be able to. Amelia fought like a wild cat, screaming words no lady should know, let alone speak.

At that moment, Hale appeared, quickly took stock, and managed to assist Ethel in restraining her sister. Meanwhile, I clambered out of the pond, no doubt covered in gross, slimy things and with magnificent bruises to add to my growing collection.

"Ophelia!" Hale called.

"I'm alright." I waved him off. "Just keep her restrained. And someone needs to call the police."

"Already done," Aunt Butty said, panting slightly as she hustled toward us. "I had Jarvis ring them when I realized what you were about."

"Sister, I cannot believe you did this," Ethel said, clearly shaken. "Why? Why would you do this?"

"I did what I had to," Amelia snapped, "since you clearly would not. I'm only sorry I didn't finish what I started."

In the distance a siren wailed.

Chapter 18

"Good gosh, I'd have never imagined one of the Kettington sisters as a spy and murderer," Chaz said over a glass of champagne.

It was the Saturday after Amelia Kettington had been arrested and we were all gathered in the ballroom at Wit's End. Harry had decided to go ahead with the party and it was no astonishment that several invitees who'd previously made excuses suddenly found themselves able to attend. Scandal does draw a crowd.

"Poor Ethel," Aunty Butty said, "she must be simply aghast."

"But why did she do it? Amelia, I mean," Miss Semple asked. She had been right behind Aunt Butty on her charge down the lawn and had seen everything, so we'd had to clue her in.

"Amelia always played the sweet innocent sister," I said. "That was her role, if you will. Ethel was always so vocal about her dissatisfaction in life that Amelia felt she'd nothing to say. I think early on, she was probably just fine with the way things were. They'd a cozy home, enough money they could live—albeit simply—without too much worry, and they didn't have to prance around the village and make appearances. No one expected anything of them. She could do what she liked, which was to sit at home knitting or reading."

"Well, something must have changed that," Chaz said, downing his champagne and snagging a glass off the tray of a passing waiter. In the background, couples whirled around the ballroom as Hale and his band, newly arrived from Paris via London, played a lively jazz tune.

"That something was Ethel," I said. "All that dissatisfaction eventually rubbed off and Amelia started wondering what life would have been like if they still had their money, their home. She was especially upset that her sister was so unhappy. I don't think she ever really understood that Ethel is the sort of person that derives pleasure from being unhappy."

"Known a few of those in my lifetime," Aunt Butty muttered.

"I've an aunt like that," Miss Semple agreed. "Ghastly. But go on, Ophelia."

"Well," I took a sip of my own champagne. I'd have preferred a cocktail. "Ethel admitted she was approached several months ago by a man calling himself Barker and purporting to be from some big manufacturing firm in America who wanted to spy on one of Harry deVane's businesses. He promised to pay a good deal of money, but she found the idea of spying distasteful and turned him down. Amelia decided then and there that since her sister was so unhappy with their circumstances, yet refused to do anything about it, she would. So she went after Barker and volunteered."

"Was there ever a German spy?" Chaz asked.

I laughed. "Actually, no. It really was just a case of industrial espionage. One of Harry's American competitors wanted information on his businesses. Simple as that."

"That explains the break-in," Miss Semple said. I hadn't told them the truth about that.

"American. Don't suppose that Mathew Breverman had anything to do with it? I see he's not here tonight," Chaz said.

"Actually, yes," I said. "Harry finally admitted to Detective Inspector Willis that he had invited Breverman because he planned to try and get information about Breverman's business from *him*. When the company documents went missing, he didn't want Breverman to know, so he lied about it. He had no idea Breverman was behind the theft. Willis dragged Breverman off to jail this afternoon."

"Banner day for him," Aunt Butty said dryly.

"What about Chamberlain's visit?" Chaz asked. "And the papers you found burned in the grate?"

"Apparently, it really was a total coincidence and nothing whatsoever to do with the theft." I had promised Harry I wouldn't tell anyone that he'd burned the documents Neville Chamberlain had brought just to be safe. He wouldn't tell me what was in the documents, and I was guessing maybe it really did have something to do with Germany.

"But why did Amelia Kettington murder that man?" Miss Semple asked.

"Her handler, Barker? Because she was angry. He refused to pay her." Because Binky had got there first and swiped the documents. "So she lured him to the house, claiming she had found further information, and killed him."

"And, like you said, she thought you were close to discovering the truth, so she tried to kill you," Chaz said. "Surprisingly strong, that woman. Hale said he had a devil of a time restraining her, even with Ethel's help."

"What will happen to her now?" Miss Semple asked.

"I imagine she'll go to prison where she belongs," Aunt Butty said tartly. "They may hang her."

"Or lock her up in Bedlam," I murmured. She had seemed rather deranged at the end.

"I, for one, am relieved it's over," Chaz said.

"Agreed. Shall we dance?" Miss Semple asked, threading her arm through Chaz's.

"Sounds delightful," he said gallantly, draining his glass before escorting her on to the dance floor.

"Ophelia, there you are." Varant appeared at my side. "I wanted to let you know, Maddie was released and she's upstairs getting some rest."

"Thank goodness. Thank you, Var—Peter. It means a great deal to me that you helped her."

He gave me a meaningful look. "I'm glad."

"Speaking of rest," Aunt Butty said, "I think we should get away for a bit, don't you, Ophelia?"

"What do you mean?"

"I'm getting itchy feet. I think we need an adventure."

I stared at her aghast. "This wasn't an adventure?"

"No, dear. This is Devon." She patted my cheek. "Think about it." She sauntered away to rope Harry into a dance.

"Care to dance, Ophelia?" Varant's eyes were dark and alluring as he led me to the dance floor, but it was Hale who I watched as the clock ticked toward midnight.

It was late, the party winding down, many of the locals having taken their leave to find their own beds. The musicians were done for the night, but someone had put on the gramophone and Al Bowlly crooned "Love Is the Sweetest Thing."

Moonlight beckoned so I stepped onto the veranda, inhaling the scent of roses and lavender. Above, the stars twinkled, and a night bird called, its haunting song echoing across the lawn.

"I was waiting for you." A shadow detached from other shadows and Hale stepped toward me.

I moved out of the sightline of anyone watching from within the house. "I wondered where you'd got to."

He reached out and pulled me against him, wrapping me close and leaning down to kiss me. His kiss was everything.

He finally pulled away. "For a moment, I thought I'd lost you. That woman—"

"Pish posh," I said airily. "I had everything under control." More or less.

He gave me a look that spoke volumes.

"All right, perhaps not *that* under control. Thank you for playing the gallant knight."

He grinned. "Any time. Just perhaps keep your duels with old ladies to a minimum."

"Not promising anything, but I'll try." I sighed and leaned against him. I'd no idea where this was going, but for now I was in the moment. And I meant to enjoy every bit of it. "Where are you off to next?" Because I'd no doubt he would be off. He was a musician. It was what he did.

"Back to Paris for a bit. The Hot Club de France has asked us to play for them. Then down to Nice. There's a club there run by an American ex-pat. We'll be there for a least a couple months."

"Sounds marvelous. I do hope you have a wonderful time."

"I'd have a better time if you were with me."

That he felt that way, and was willing to admit it, warmed the very cockles of my heart. "Well, you never know. Mayhap Father Christmas will come early."

Later that night I barged into Aunt Butty's room, startling her half to death. "Aunt, you're right. Let's go on an adventure."

She lifted a brow as she set aside her novel. "Do you have a particular place in mind?"

I grinned. "I might…"

The End

Note from the Author

Thank you for reading. If you enjoyed this book, I'd appreciate it if you'd help others find it so they can enjoy it too.

- Lend it: This e-book is lending-enabled, so feel free to share it with your friends, readers' groups, and discussion boards.

- Review it: Let other potential readers know what you liked or didn't like about the story.

- Sign Up: Join in on the fun on Shéa's email list: https://www.subscribepage.com/cozymystery

Book updates can be found at www.sheamacleod.com

About Shéa MacLeod

Shéa MacLeod is the author of the bestselling paranormal series, Sunwalker Saga, as well as the award nominated cozy mystery series Viola Roberts Cozy Mysteries. She has dreamed of writing novels since before she could hold a crayon. She totally blames her mother.

She resides in the leafy green hills outside Portland, Oregon where she indulges in her fondness for strong coffee, Ancient Aliens reruns, lemon curd, and dragons. She can usually be found at her desk dreaming of ways to kill people (or vampires). Fictionally speaking, of course.

Other Books by Shéa MacLeod

Lady Rample Mysteries
Lady Rample Steps Out
Lady Rample Spies a Clue
Lady Rample and the Silver Screen (coming soon)

Viola Roberts Cozy Mysteries
The Corpse in the Cabana
The Stiff in the Study
The Poison in the Pudding
The Body in the Bathtub
The Venom in the Valentine
The Remains in the Rectory
The Death in the Drink

Notting Hill Diaries
To Kiss a Prince
Kissing Frogs
Kiss Me, Chloe
Kiss Me, Stupid
Kissing Mr. Darcy

Cupcake Goddess Novelettes
Be Careful What You Wish For
Nothing Tastes As Good
Soulfully Sweet
A Stich in Time

Omicron ZX
Omicron Zed-X: Omicron ZX
A Rage of Angels

Dragon Wars
Dragon Warrior
Dragon Lord
Dragon Goddess
Green Witch
Dragon Corps
Dragon Mage
Dragon's Angel

Sunwalker Saga
Kissed by Blood
Kissed by Darkness
Kissed by Fire
Kissed by Smoke
Kissed by Moonlight
Kissed by Ice
Kissed by Eternity
Kissed by Destiny

Sunwalker Saga: Soulshifter Trilogy
Fearless
Haunted
Soulshifter

Sunwalker Saga: Witch Blood Series
Spellwalker
Deathwalker
Mistwalker
Dreamwalker

Made in the USA
Middletown, DE
08 February 2020